THE SECRET OF THE SCARLET RIBBON

A Kitty Hawkins Adventure

Justin Strain grew up in Portsmouth and served in the Royal Navy before retraining as a physiotherapist. He still lives in Portsmouth with his wife and two children and, when he is not working or writing, he enjoys playing the violin and messing around on boats.

Justin Strain

THE SECRET OF THE SCARLET RIBBON

A Kitty Hawkins Adventure

LITTLE WORLD PUBLISHING

Portsmouth

Published by Little World 2017

All characters in this book are entirely fictional with the exceptions of Charles Dickens and John Pounds. Any other resemblance to any real characters is unintended. Many of the places and events in this book are historical however some have been altered for artistic purposes. The map on page 6 was prepared using contemporary maps accessed by kind permission of Portsmouth City Libraries.

ISBN 978-0-9932809-3-1

For my mum.

Thanks for all the help along the way.

With special thanks to my proof-readers,

Eva and Robbie.

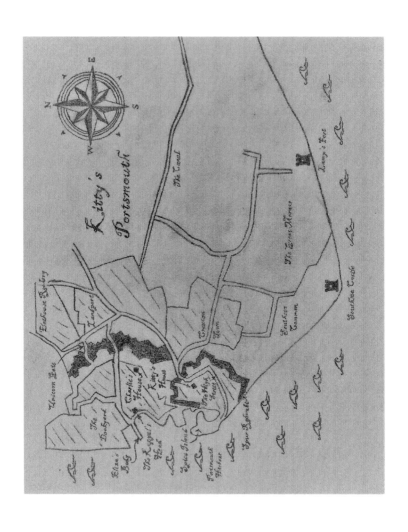

1831

Portsmouth

Chapter 1

Kitty Hawkins pushed a lock of ginger hair
out of her eyes and looked up at the
gentleman on the dappled grey horse. He was
a toff. You could tell that from his smartly
tailored black suit and top hat. His clothing
lent him an air of age and experience but on
closer inspection the soft cheeks and sparse
moustache revealed his youth. He looked
down and tossed a small coin in her direction.
Kitty caught it deftly. She eyed the man
suspiciously. Toffs didn't just throw you
money for no reason. Some people have a
nose for trouble, and Kitty's nose was
twitching frantically.

"What do you want, mister?"

The toff seemed amused by her insolence.

"Listen girl, there's more where that came
from if you can help me. You seem like a
sharp lass who knows her way around."

Kitty was unimpressed by the compliments. It usually meant someone was going to ask you to do something you didn't want to do. She had a brief urge to grab the penny and run, but she couldn't help feeling a little curious as to what he would ask of her. Besides, he'd soon catch her on that horse and then she'd really be in trouble.

"So, say I can help you, what's the business then."

She fought to keep her face impassive, despite her rising excitement.

"Information. And I want you to keep your eyes open. I'm looking for a lady. Her name is Eliza Pemberton. She is thirty-two years of age and has recently travelled here from London. She stands about five and a half feet tall and has auburn hair, much like yours. There's plenty of other people looking for her too. It's vital that I find her first. My name is Peabody. Samuel Peabody. If you find her, bring her to me and I'll double what I've paid you. You'll find me at the Keppel's Head Hotel."

The gentleman spurred his horse and rode away from her. Kitty looked after him, almost impressed, despite herself.

The street was crowded with people. Kitty threaded her way through the crowd, taking care not to bump into anyone. It wouldn't be the first time she'd been accused (wrongly) of thieving. She didn't want to take any chances.

She crossed the road over to the camber, stepping carefully over the sewage that flowed slowly down its middle. Soon the stench of excrement was overwhelmed by the stench of fish. The traders had been selling for hours, shouting lustily to anyone passing, "Fish! Fish! Luvverly fish!"

The 'luvverly' fish lay forlornly in the bottoms of their crates, their upturned eyes staring unblinking into the late morning sun. Their scales had lost the wet gleam of the freshly landed catch and were encrusted in a drying film. Those that were left smelt increasingly putrid and Kitty wrinkled her nose in distaste as she passed. The weary fishmongers sprayed them ineffectually with water to slow their decay, but as the droplets landed they evaporated under the harsh sun. At the back end of the fish-market the crowds thinned and Kitty gathered pace, dancing nimbly between the discarded remains of the fish-hauls and the market detritus. A couple of sailors smiled at her as she ran past.

"Kitty! Kitty! There you are."

She stopped and turned towards the friendly voice.

At fourteen years of age, Charlie Miller was a few month's older than her, but slight and no more than her in height. His mud-spattered face turned to hers and he smiled, showing the gap where he was missing a tooth. She'd often asked him how he'd lost the tooth but he never told her. He just laughed and shrugged his shoulders.

"Where've you been Kitty? Mr Pounds' been asking for you."

Kitty felt a twinge of guilt as she thought of Mr Pounds looking for her. She was not the only one to miss a class. Most of them did from time to time. But she knew he had a soft spot for her, and she hated to let him down.

"I'll come now. There's still a bit of time. I had things to do this morning."

She didn't tell Charlie about the man on the horse, or her new mission. She wasn't sure why, but she wanted to keep it secret a little while longer.

They raced further inland, away from the smells and sounds of the fishmarket. As they approached Mr Pounds' workshop Kitty saw the familiar gaggle of children crowded around the open doors. In the middle of the shop Mr Pounds sat, working intently upon an old shoe, while talking continuously to the children clustered around him. He didn't look at her as she approached, but his voice caught her.

"Ah, Kitty. I was wondering what's become of you. You hungry then?"

Without seeming to look, he fired towards her, with great accuracy a small projectile from within the folds of his cloak. Kitty caught the baked potato gratefully.

"Thank you, Mr Pounds. I'm famished."

Kitty settled down to eat her potato, savouring the oily heat as it lightly seared the inside of her mouth. The children were practising their arithmetic. Mr Pounds fired questions at them from his central seat, carefully tailoring the difficulty to the boy or girl they were aimed at. A correct answer brought a smile and a compliment. The wrong answer brought a frown, but the frown had no depth behind it, and the friendly eyes gave away his good humour.

Occasionally the children would struggle and Mr Pounds would patiently explain whatever they were working on. It was all so familiar to Kitty. It felt as much like home as the tiny house she shared with her parents.

Often Mr Pounds would pretend to pick on Kitty, saving his toughest questions for her.

Kitty didn't mind. She could usually answer them and she quite enjoyed the attention. But today he seemed somehow to know that things were different. Somehow the old cobbler sensed her need for solitude, and he left her alone to ponder over the mystery of the missing lady.

It certainly was a mystery. Kitty was not used to wealthy strangers accosting her like this. She was caught between distrust and intrigue, but intrigue was gradually getting the upper hand. She looked across at Charlie. He had settled quickly into the lesson and was joining in loudly with the game of sums, squealing with laughter when Mr Pounds caught him, or one of the other children, out. Kitty smiled. She liked Charlie. She'd known him as long as she could remember. His mother was a seamstress and his father a sailor. Charlie didn't see much of his father. He was away at sea a lot, and when he was back he was mostly drunk. Kitty didn't think Charlie or his mum were sorry to wave him goodbye.

As the lesson ended, Charlie and Kitty wandered out into the afternoon sun. It was a hot day and the paving baked beneath their feet.

"What are you doing now?"

Charlie's question was loaded with expectation. Whatever she was doing, Charlie would want to be there. He would have his own work to do. Their parents would tolerate them going to their lessons, as long as they spent the rest of the day bringing in some money. But she knew Charlie would mildly resent the hours he spent rooting for money in the muck. Kitty's spirits brightened. She already had a shilling. She'd made her day's money before she started.

"I've got a mission Charlie. Do you want to help me?"

Again Charlie's smile split his face.

"What is it Kitty? Can you tell me?"

Kitty laughed and told him about the toff and the lady with the auburn hair. Charlie looked a bit doubtful.

"It's not much to go, on is it Kitty? I mean, there's more than one lady with auburn hair. You, for instance."

He looked around him, as if half-expecting to see a sudden surge of auburn-haired ladies descending on them.

"I know Charlie. It's not much to go on. But that's all he told me. Her name is Eliza Pemberton. His name is Samuel Peabody. And if we find her then there'll be money in it for both of us."

***

Smog was settling on Portsea as Kitty returned home. She could hear the sounds of industry from the dockyard in the background and the air hung heavy in the heat of the day. The house was small, and faced onto a shared cobbled courtyard. Already the glass of the windows had picked up the morning's dust. As she swung the door open her mother looked up expectantly.

"Ah, Kitty love, come to help your mother. You're always such a good daughter."

Kitty shifted uncomfortably. She knew she ought to give her mother the shilling but reluctance overcame obedience. Besides, if she did, she would have to explain where she got it, and she wasn't ready to tell her parents about her mission.

"Kitty, your father's prepared a new load. There, in the corner. You can package them up to sell this afternoon."

Kitty looked at the neatly stacked candles in the corner. Each one was smooth and rounded where the tallow had been dipped and hardened. The small bundles were carefully bound to make them easier to carry. Kitty stuffed a dozen of the bundles into a bag. She could come back for more if she sold them all. Dutifully Kitty hoisted the bag onto her shoulder. She crossed to her mother and kissed her on the cheek. Her mother's hand caught hers and for a moment squeezed with surprising vigour. The watery eyes held hers for a few silent seconds.

"Be careful my love. Come back soon, and safe."

And then the spell was broken, and Kitty was stepping back out into the bustle of the street. After a moment's deliberation, Kitty headed for the market, carrying the bag carefully. She knew how hard her father worked to craft the candles and that alone made them precious.

As she reached the Hard she smiled at a newspaper boy, lustily advertising the day's stories to passers-by at the top of his voice. He grinned back at her before turning to ply his trade with an elderly gentleman in a suit. The market was still busy with people, although many of the stalls were depleted from the morning's trading. It wasn't hard to find a space, next to a tired looking coffee seller, who looked like he had been there since the early hours. Kitty spread her cotton blanket across the paving and arranged the candles in as attractive a display as she could manage. Across the road she glanced up at

15

the Keppel's Head hotel, towering above her, and thought of Mr Peabody and her mission.

***

Charlie smiled at the warm sensation of sludge squelching between his toes. The spring tide had receded leaving the virgin mud fresh and exposed. The recent storm had thrown up hitherto lost treasures from the seabed. It was rich pickings for the mud-larks. [1]

Above them the dock wall thronged with people – a ready supply for the fortunate scavenger. With each movement of his feet the stench emanating from the mire briefly intensified, then faded into the background. He looked down at the small collection in his hands: a couple of pennies, nothing more in terms of coin; a stained and corroded brass ring, but with a bit of effort it could shine up well; a couple of assorted bits of metal, not worth much but they might come in useful. All in all, it wasn't a bad haul. Not the best, but he'd had a lot worse.

---

[1] Mud-lark: Someone who searches for treasure in the mud-flats of harbours, canals or rivers.

Charlie looked around at his fellow mud-larks. A couple of them had started a brief mud-slinging contest a bit further out, closer to the deeper water. He smiled indulgently. It looked like fun but they weren't going to find any prizes that way. He turned back to the mud, plunging his arms in elbow deep. The September sun was drying the surface, leaving a thin crust which crumbled quickly beneath his fingers, allowing them to penetrate to the cooler, softer layers beneath, where the infiltrating water had remained trapped. These were the rich layers. This was where the treasures lay, unseen from above, awaiting the lucky finder.

It wasn't just luck though. Charlie was proud of his skill. He could see the miniscule depressions on the surface that indicated where it had been previously punctured. His fingers and toes had eyes of their own, feeling for the changes in muddy texture where the seabed held its secrets close. It wasn't a glamorous job, but it was what he was good at.

The tide would still be ebbing for a few hours. Charlie worked quickly. This was when the harbour was at its most generous, still fresh and unspoilt by the feet and hands of the grubbing children. He worked at the edge, where the water still lapped, scouring the seabed as soon as it became visible.

As he worked Charlie thought about Kitty and her auburn-haired lady. He wouldn't say it to Kitty, but she would be hard to find. She could be anywhere in the city, or out of it for that matter. Still, if she was in the city there was no-one better to find her than a mud-lark. After all, finding things was what they were good at.

***

The sun hung low in the sky as Kitty finished. She looked out over the water. Soft red light rippled across the surface. The water was returning and the mud gradually receded as the sea reclaimed its territory, wiping clean the marks of the mud-larks. The other children had left, hoarding their treasures jealously as their feet found the firm foundation of the dock wall. One small, lonely figure still stood out in the mud-flats, silently defying the gently lapping approach of the advancing tide. Charlie always worked longest. Charlie always worked latest.

In the middle of the harbour a ship lay at anchor, its sails bundled tightly to the wooden spars and the anchor chain rattling occasionally with the gentle movement of the water. Charlie glanced at the ship and looked away. His father had been gone for several months and he didn't know when he would return. The absence didn't bother him. It was the return he feared. Tearing his mind away, he bent to his task. He didn't have much time left before the tide pushed him back to shore. But this was the time he enjoyed the most. When the others had gone and he could be left with his own thoughts. It was a special time. He glanced up at the dockside and saw Kitty. He waved and she waved back. He never minded Kitty being there. She didn't intrude on his thoughts. Or if she did, it was in a good way. She had a knack of just being there, being part of the picture, without disturbing it. She could stay.

Eventually he made his way over to where Kitty sat - his haul for the day complete, if not extensive. He hauled himself onto the quayside and wiped the worst of the grime on the edge of the wall. He sat, legs dangling against the rough stonework, breathing in large gulps of the harbour air, loaded with the sulphuric smell of the mud that coated him.

"There's always tomorrow Kitty."

Kitty wondered if he had sensed her disappointment. She had been sure they

would find the lady. It wasn't about the money. It was the intrigue that captivated her.
"I know Charlie. Thanks for trying."
"I did try Kitty. I really did."
He was keen to tell her of his efforts and Kitty didn't have the heart to deny him.
"I've told the other lads to keep a lookout. Nobody's seen anything, but if anyone can find her, they can."
Kitty stifled a mild sense of annoyance. She'd been happy to tell Charlie. He was her friend. But she hadn't wanted her secret shared.
"Why did you tell them Charlie? You shouldn't have done that. I never said you could."
She realised as she said it that she'd never said he couldn't either.
"Look Kitty, you know how things work. Between the two of us we'll never find her. We need more eyes, more ears. I could've kept it to myself, but this way I can cover half of Portsmouth."
Kitty looked out across the water. It occurred to her that she didn't know why they were looking for the lady. She didn't know anything much really. She just knew that it was her mystery and she wanted to solve it.

"That's ok Charlie. It's a good idea. You're right. We can't do this on our own."

They sat enjoying the quietening evening. The street stalls had packed up and the noise of traders had died down. Residual smells mingled in the air from the depleted market. The taverns were starting to pick up trade but it was not late enough yet for raucousness. Eventually Kitty stood. She would have to head home soon. She was exhausted from the day's labour. Charlie stood with her.

"Come on Charlie, let's head back. We won't find anything more tonight."

She nearly said that their parents would be waiting but realised with a pang of pity that Charlie's probably wouldn't be.

Charlie paused, somehow unwilling to leave. He looked out to where the tide still lapped invitingly at the dwindling mud-banks. The rotten timbers of the small pier protruded from the seabed like a tangled mesh of gnarled tree-roots. Some of the timbers had fallen, horizontally onto the mud, and lay like fallen soldiers around the vertical pillars. The sea had pulled a few of them away, but most still clung to the lattice framework they came from.

Something looked different. Charlie could not quite say what, but he realised that it had been nagging at him all afternoon. Something didn't quite fit. He had been too busy to pay it any mind earlier, too intent on his scavenging. But now the feeling nagged at him all the more, like an itch, just beyond the scratching reach of his fingers.

"Hang on Kitty. There's something I want to check out."

He set off, back across the mud towards the pier. Kitty marvelled at how his feet seemed to glide effortlessly over the surface. She felt a sudden lift of excitement as she watched him skate across the soft mud.

"Wait! Charlie, wait! I'm coming too!"

Charlie laughed.

"Kitty Hawkins, you're crazy. You'll get yourself filthy."

But Kitty could see the delight on his face as he came back to help her. She scrambled over the dock wall and shuffling her legs she lowered her body gradually over until she was hanging by her fingertips. For a few moments her feet waved in space.

"You're almost there, Kitty. Let yourself drop and I'll catch you."

Trusting to Charlie's advice, Kitty let go, and felt her feet sink into soft mud. The mud held her feet fast, and Charlie's arm caught her around the shoulders and stopped her falling.

She looked across the rippling water. She couldn't see anything different, but Charlie seemed certain and trustingly she followed after him. Charlie looked back at her and grinned.

"You're in the mud-larks' world now Kitty!" They both waded slowly further into the mud. It stank, and Kitty gagged on the powerful stench. She could feel the damp soak into her trousers and the sludge grate against her knees. On two occasions she felt something move beneath her and had to stifle a scream. The mud sucked at her legs, resisting every wallowing step. She could feel sweat mingling with the muck she was coated in. When they reached the water's edge Kitty stopped. Charlie smiled at her encouragingly. She was undeniably impressed by how little effect the pervasive mud seemed to have on him. Her usual confidence had deserted her in this morass of stinking muck. Charlie pointed under the pier.

"Look, Kitty, there, in the middle. It looks like a log, but it isn't. It's too rounded. And it's not fallen like the others. It looks to me like it's been washed up by the tide and got tangled under here."

Kitty looked where Charlie was pointing and

realised that he was right. One of the logs did look out of place.

"I'm going in."

Charlie dived under the pier, deftly weaving between the fallen lumps of wood. She watched him wade up to his thighs. Shortly after he stopped and hissed back.

"This is it! I'll pull it back to you."

"No, wait. I'll help you."

Kitty followed him into the jungle of rotting wood, encrusted with tiny sea creatures and draped in slimy seaweed. She had thought the smell of the mud was bad enough, but in the dark spaces under the jetty it was positively pungent. She shuddered and, squaring her shoulders, struck out for where she could just about see Charlie in the dim light.

The bundle was heavy and it took them a few minutes to drag it through the water. Eventually, after much heaving and panting, they pulled it out onto the open mudflats.

Even close up it was hard to see what the bundle was. It was coated in thick mud and the dusk twilight obscured their sight further. Kitty reached out and felt the familiar roughness of a hessian sack. She tugged at the sack to open it, but to no avail. She heaved harder, clenching her jaw with the effort. She looked up at Charlie. He was sitting in the mud, breathing heavily.

"Well come on then. Are you going to help here, or what?"

Charlie nodded silently and pulled a knife from his belt. It took a matter of seconds to slit open the sack and reveal the contents. Despite herself, Kitty retched as she saw the tangled mass of red hair. Charlie stared in shocked silence at the bag.

It was a woman. She was dead. Kitty was sure of that. She had been pretty. You could still see a cheerful, friendly face beneath the waxen pallor of death. Kitty thought she would have been fun to know. Her clothes were good quality. Not necessarily rich, but certainly not poor. The body was fairly fresh. It didn't smell putrid yet. Kitty had seen dead bodies before and knew the smell of an old one.

As she stared in the gloom at the body, a break in the cloud shone a sudden shaft of moonlight across it. Magically illuminated, Kitty looked more closely at the beautiful, mysterious lady, imagining her laughing, singing, her auburn curls swept up and neatly arranged, not strewn dishevelled across her face. She looked up at Charlie.

"What shall we do? We'd better call the police."

"Are you mad?" Charlie stared at her, leaving her in no doubt as to his opinion. "They'll never believe us. We'll be clapped in gaol before you know it! I say we leave her here and pretend as we've never seen her. We can't help her, anyway."

Kitty looked doubtful.

"But we must tell someone, surely? We can't just leave her."

"Yes we can. They'll find her tomorrow anyway, out in the open like this. And best we're a long way away when they do."

Kitty was unconvinced but didn't argue with him anymore.

She glanced once more at the beautiful lady, and stopped. There, caught in the moon's soft glow, but clear to see as the hair tumbled away from the shoulder, a small silver locket glistened against her chest. Kitty picked the locket up and examined it closely. It was plain on the outside, but sprang open easily to reveal a picture of a young boy, and the ornately engraved initials,

E.P.

"Those... those initials," she whispered hoarsely, "EP – Eliza Pemberton. Charlie! Charlie! Don't you see? It's her! The woman we were looking for! It's her!"

Charlie clearly did see, and looked at the corpse with renewed animation. Kitty felt a fleeting sadness pass over her. She reached out and plucked the locket from the lady's breast. Kitty thought for a moment and then started to check the lady's garments and pockets for anything else.

"What are you doing?" asked Charlie. "You can't steal from a dead person."

"I'm not stealing Charlie. Like you say, she's dead anyway. But there might be a clue - something, anything - to tell us why they were looking for her."

She went over the woman's body quickly, but as carefully as she could. She had no purse on her. Kitty guessed that whoever killed her must have taken it. But whatever they had wanted with her, it had not been robbery. She still had all her jewellery – the locket, a bracelet, and two rings. Kitty stared at the jewels. They were worth more than her family would have in a week. She looked at Charlie. She could tell he was tempted too, but he shook his head. Kitty realised he was right. She couldn't steal from a dead person.

She looked at the lady's hands. The left one was open, displaying her rings to the night. The right hand was clenched tightly into a fist, as if she had been desperately trying to cling to something when she died. Kitty carefully prised the stiff fingers open to see what they were holding. In the lady's open palm lay a small scarlet ribbon. It was stuck with a pin, like a brooch, but the ribbon was twisted in a pattern, almost like the legs and body of a person. She turned it over in her hand, and then thoughtfully tucked it away in her own pocket.

"I wonder why she was killed." whispered Charlie.

"I don't know. We'll have to ask Mr Peabody."

"Can we trust him, do you think?"

Kitty thought about the question. She didn't know him, other than their one chance meeting on the street. How could she trust him? But then again what other choices did they have?

"I think we'll have to trust him Charlie. He's the only one that can help us. Let's go and see him…"

"… tomorrow, Kitty." Charlie finished the sentence for her. "Let's go and see him tomorrow. We can't do anything for this lady

now, and it's getting dark already. Your
parents will be wondering where you are. My
mother…" he laughed derisively, "… my
mother will be wondering where her money
is."

Kitty reluctantly agreed. She was still eager
to see Mr Peabody, but it was getting late.

"Should we tell our parents, do you think?"

Charlie shrugged.

"What's the point? At best they won't believe
us. At worst they'll tan our hides for it. You
can tell yours if you like but I'm keeping
quiet."

***

They didn't go straight home. There was no
particular reason for it, but neither of them
felt tired, despite the late hour. Reluctant to
end the excitement of the evening, their feet
carried them along the High Street, towards
the camber dock.

The sky was an inky purple-black, lit only by
the soft glow of the gas-lamps and the
fulsome moon ahead of them. Silhouetted
against the moon's white orb, an owl glided
silently through the night, coming to rest in
the spidery branches of an aged and leafless
tree.

They could hear the increasingly rowdy noise from Spice Island in the background. Kitty looked at Charlie.

"What do you think it all means?"

"I don't know Kitty, I don't know. But I don't like it. I mean, that lady - someone killed her, didn't they? She didn't get into the mud by accident. And if we get mixed up in it, what's to stop them coming after us as well? Whoever's behind this…"

Kitty stopped suddenly, at the corner of Penny Street. Charlie broke off mid-sentence and stared at her.

"Kitty, what is it?"

"Shhhhhh!"

Kitty strained her ears to hear. She had been dimly conscious of someone lurking in the darkened street, but had not bothered to pay it any heed. Not until she heard one word that grabbed her attention.

"Peabody."

Chapter 2

Charlie and Kitty flattened themselves against the corner wall and peered down Penny Street. About a third of the way down they could see a couple of figures. It was too dark to see them clearly but Kitty assumed they were men from their voices. They were muttering to each other, but the words were mumbled and impossible to make out. Occasionally Kitty would catch the odd snatch of a phrase.

"… Mr Chamberlain'll be pleased to learn of this…"

"… pay me handsomely I hope…"

Kitty was intrigued but neither of them dared encroach down the gloomy street for fear of being seen. The men's conversation was animated, but hushed. They had been talking a few minutes when Kitty, straining forward to hear better, felt her foot slip and heard the sound of a stone scuffing beneath her. Instantly the men looked up and Kitty and Charlie shrank back, scarcely daring to breathe. The men looked furtively around the dark street. They waited like this for what seemed like an age, until eventually the men seemed to be satisfied and started to walk away from them. Charlie looked questioningly at Kitty. She nodded and, quietly and carefully they sneaked along the lane in stealthy pursuit.

The men were not hurrying and Charlie and Kitty had no problem keeping up with them. As their eyes adjusted to the dark Kitty could make out their shapes more clearly - one tall and spindly, the other shorter, more thick set. At the bottom of Penny Street the forbidding shape of the gaol loomed above them in the darkness. A field led away from the gaol, towards the esplanade, and the two men crossed into it.

The night was darkening and the children blended into the shadow of the brewery. On the other side of the field was a raised rampart of earth towards which the two men made their way. Kitty and Charlie watched as they disappeared into a dark tunnel leading through the rampart.

"I know that tunnel. It leads through to the Spur Redoubt."

As the men disappeared, Kitty and Charlie broke out of the shadows and raced towards the dark passageway. Creeping in they could just see the men at the other end. The tunnel was gloomy and damp, lit only by the low glow of the moon and the gas lamps on the esplanade. They hardly dared to breathe, as the faintest sound seemed to echo along the cold, wet stones. In the distance, the men had emerged into the night, and Kitty briefly saw them, captured in the circular glow of the tunnel opening, before they moved out of view.

Kitty shivered. It was cold, but it was the sense of danger that made her hair stand on end. They crept cautiously to the edge of the tunnel, hoping the men weren't waiting for them. Without warning, Charlie grabbed Kitty's arm. She started but made no sound. Charlie put a finger to his lips and pointed with his other hand. Ahead of them a wooden drawbridge stretched, spanning the moat between the tunnel's end and the Spur Redoubt opposite. The drawbridge was sturdy but overgrown, a tangled mass of creepers covering the thick tar that coated it. Following Charlie's hand, Kitty saw that their quarry had reached the redoubt on the other side of the drawbridge and seemed to have stopped, as if waiting for something.

The Spur Redoubt was an ancient fortification, long disused and now surrounded mainly by bathing machines for intrepid bathers, keen to soak in the cleansing salts of the sea. Much of the fort's stonework was still in place and a small sallyport to its side remained, providing a landing stage for boats to take sailors to their waiting ships. Kitty's father had often talked of how he had waved farewell to Admiral Nelson at the Spur Redoubt as he took ship for Trafalgar. Her mother always rolled her eyes at this story and Kitty couldn't help but doubt whether her father had really been there. Since Nelson's day, the redoubt and its sallyport were little used, save for the bathers that swarmed there in the summer.

Tonight, however, there was clearly business afoot. Straining her ears, Kitty could hear the faint splash of oars in the water. A boat was approaching. She peered into the gloom but could see nothing. The boat was not displaying any lights, and the occasional voices she heard were low and muffled. Whoever they were, they were not keen to advertise their presence.

Suddenly the clouds broke and, for a brief moment, the two men they had been following were clearly silhouetted by the rising moon. They stood, looking out to sea, where Kitty could now see a tiny rowing boat, making its way effortfully to the landing stage. The boat was crewed by two sailors, but another figure sat in the middle, oddly

shapeless but roughly man-sized. Kitty
looked quizzically at Charlie who shrugged
his shoulders in reply.

Slowly and cautiously the little boat fought
the tide to the short wooden jetty where the
men were waiting. Kitty heard muffled
voices calling and saw one of the men catch
the boat's rope. A few moments later they
saw something bundled from the boat onto the
landing stage, falling with a thud at the taller
man's foot. The man looked down with
distaste and laid a forceful kick into the
middle of the bundle. The bundle groaned.
Charlie gasped next to Kitty and she laid a
gentle hand on his arm. The bundle was a
person!

The shorter man joined in, kicking sharp,
jabbing thrusts at the prisoner, but backing
away immediately after, as if shocked by his
own audacity. The taller man put his arm out
and his companion stopped. They stooped to
the bundle and pulled it roughly to its feet.
The prisoner was surprisingly tall, the shape
of a large man, Kitty thought. He staggered a
few times and groaned again. The groan was
deep and rich, and the sound carried clearly in
the night air. That earned him another kick
and he stumbled, almost to one knee, and then
recovered. Kitty could see that, whoever it

was, his head was obscured by a hessian sack. His arms were tied behind his back, and he wandered precariously from side to side as he moved, almost falling off the jetty, until another well-aimed kick brought him back to the centre. Eventually the three of them moved off the jetty and the strange procession made their way eastwards, along the seafront. Kitty made to follow them but Charlie held her back. She looked at him angrily.

"Come on! They're getting away."

Charlie seemed reluctant, but eventually he followed. The two men, pushing their prisoner between them, continued their tantalisingly slow progress along the shoreline. Cloud swallowed the moon once more and in the darkness the two children padded after them.

"I don't like this. Not one bit. We're in over our heads Kitty."

"Hssst! Quit your moaning!"

Kitty's whisper was quiet but forceful. She glared invisibly at Charlie in the dark.

"Come on, we've got to keep up with them!"

They hurried on in their pursuit, just about keeping the dark shapes in view. As they crept away from the town the dark deepened. Kitty could swear she saw other shapes loom about them, although she knew there was nothing there. But the mind and the dark conspired to trick the thoughts and Kitty gave an involuntary shudder. Charlie seemed to sense her disquiet.

"You okay Kitty?"

Kitty nodded, and then, realising how futile that was, hissed,

"Yes."

They had gone maybe half a mile when, without warning, the clouds parted and allowed the moon's light a clear, unencumbered path. Bathed suddenly in its blue-white glow, Kitty and Charlie sank immediately to the ground. As they did so the taller man turned and for a split-second Kitty could have sworn she looked straight into his darkly malevolent eyes. The eyes stared, yellow and round, for a brief moment, then blinked and looked away.

The men continued onwards, and soon disappeared into the murky darkness. Kitty and Charlie stayed, still and silent, watching them vanish. It was several minutes before either spoke. Kitty was shaken by the glare of the man's eyes, and by their effect on her. She felt fettered by fear, her thoughts paralysed. Eventually it was Charlie that spoke, cracking the silence.

"Come on Kitty, we'd better get home."

***

1819

West Africa

The smell of burning seared the hazy African air, tainting the breath with its bitter, acrid stench. A couple of birds circled above them, waiting to feed on the charred remains of the livestock. The buzz of crickets reached a crescendo, but so constant was the sound that Lamin barely noticed it. He looked around at the devastation. The village was destroyed, but could be rebuilt. It had happened before and would happen again. Bushfires were not uncommon in the arid African plains.

The men of the village rested wearily on the makeshift tools that they had used to beat back the flames. But in the end, it had not been human endeavour but nature that had overcome the blaze. The fire had simply run its course, and died as quickly as it had arisen.

The women brought water for their men, and herded children and animals before them, salving their fear and delivering them to safety.

The parched lands all around were desolate. Smoke-blackened fields surrounded the carcasses of ruined huts. Only as the ground gave way to the watery rice fields nearer the river did the ravaging flames abate. Lamin followed his wife, Nyima, as she hustled and chided their family. Little Mamadi ran alongside her, laughing and prodding the goat with his pudgy hands. For him the fear was already forgotten. His faith in his parents was absolute and he looked back at Lamin with trusting eyes that tugged at his soul.

They made for the riverbank, and for the lush green strip of forest that ran thinly beside it. Here the emerald leaves shielded the blue ribbon of water from the surrounding dusty landscape. Little more than a mile wide in places, it harboured an abundance of life that could survive nowhere else. Lamin looked at the other villagers, also making their way to the forest. The forest would give them water. The forest would give them food. The forest would shelter them while they rebuilt their village and their lives.

As they reached the overhanging green canopy, Lamin experienced the fleeting pang of claustrophobia that he always felt as he left the open sky behind. He loved the forest, but it reminded him how small and close the world was. On the plains you could see forever, the horizon disappearing in the shimmering heat. In the forest you only saw the minutiae. Around him he could hear the rustle of his fellow villagers as they also sought refuge in the green sanctuary, but already they were unseen, hidden by the foliage. The goat bleated plaintively, giving voice to its fear and uncertainty. Mamadi stroked its back affectionately. Nyima smiled at the boy, and shifted the suckling baby at her breast. As she looked back at Lamin the smiled succumbed to apprehension.

They reached the river. Lamin sat at the edge and bathed his singed and painful skin in the cool water. The children were less restrained and splashed noisily in the shadows. Instinctively he went to quiet them, but then smiled. Let them enjoy their moment.

As he stood from the river he felt the flicker of the movement in the undergrowth and tensed, suddenly alert to danger. The children noticed and the splashing abruptly ceased. The men emerged from the bushes, rifles raised. He did not know them, but their smiles held no compassion.

***

Kitty pushed the door open quietly, hoping she could sneak in without being noticed. The embers were still glowing in the hearth, but she couldn't see anyone in the small front room. She glanced up the stairs that led to her parents' room. There was no sign or sound of movement, and slowly Kitty entered the house and made her way across the floor.

"Kitty! Where have you been! I've been worried sick about you."

Kitty's mother appeared from the small kitchen doorway at the back of the house. She rushed to her daughter and for a moment Kitty was enfolded in a warm, close embrace. The moment passed quickly and her mother shook her by the shoulders and steered her into the sewing chair in the corner.

"What were you doing? Do you realise the time? I was dreading to think what might have happened to you? Do you realise that your father has been out for hours looking for you?"

Kitty swallowed the vague sense of shame that was competing with her frustration. She knew her mother worried about her, especially these days. She understood, and she loved her mother for it. But she could look after herself. She didn't need constant cosseting.

The initial onslaught of angry affection died down for a moment. Her mother paused and took a deep breath.

"Look at you Kitty. You're filthy! What a state you are, covered in mud and wet through. What have you been doing? You'll catch a chill like that, and no mistake. Let's get you out of those wet things right away." Her mother continued to fuss and scold as she helped her out of her clothes. Kitty allowed herself to be undressed, and wrapped herself gratefully in the warm blanket her mother gave her. She was settling back into a chair under her mother's baleful gaze when the front door opened. Her father walked in looking, as ever, unflustered, but tired.

"Kitty love, there you are. See, my love, she's back safe as I said she would be. She's a smart girl, our Kitty."

Her mother hugged her again. Up close Kitty could see the faint traces of fresh tears clinging to the corners of her eyes. Again she felt a brief stab of guilt, and she kissed her mother dutifully.

"Thank the Lord you are safe, Kitty. Thank the Lord."

***

"So where were you Kitty? Really, I mean?"
Her mother had gone to bed, comforted but
still agitated.

"I told you dad, we finished late, there was
much to do. And then we took a wrong turn
down the High Street which delayed us. But
look, I earned an extra shilling."

Her father eyed her suspiciously.

"Kitty Hawkins, you know every back street
in this part of the city. You did not take a
wrong turn. You have never taken a wrong
turn. Besides which, you don't get covered
head to toe in mud just by getting lost. Now,
what have you been doing and how did you
come by this shilling?"

Kitty looked at the floor, as if suddenly
intrigued by the whirling patterns in the
warped wooden floorboards.

"Mud-larking…" she mumbled.

"Tell me again Kitty, this time loud enough
for me to hear."

"Mud-larking."

Again her father's eyes narrowed.

"With Charlie Miller by any chance?"

Kitty nodded.

"Look, Kitty lass, I know you like the lad, and
heaven knows, so do I, but you shouldn't be
scrabbling around in the mud with him.
You're better than that."

Kitty felt a sudden surge of anger.

"What do you mean, I'm better than that. He's my friend, and there's nothing wrong with what he does."

Her father relented a little.

"Oh Kitty, I'm not saying there is. Like I say he's a good lad, just unlucky with his family. And he's doing the best he can to earn a crust. But you don't need to Kitty."

Kitty nodded her acquiescence. She hated lying to her father and longed for the conversation to be over.

Her father's face relaxed slightly, although still remaining suspicious.

"Please watch yourself Kitty. I don't want you getting into anything you shouldn't be involved in."

"It's ok dad. I'll take care."

He looked searchingly at her for a moment.

"Your mother worries a lot, but she has good reason to. You know that Kitty. Please be careful."

Her father kissed her on top of her head, and slowly clambered up the steep staircase to the bedroom above. Kitty picked up her bedroll and laid it out in the corner of the room. Not too close to the hearth, but close enough to feel its warmth. She lay down and closed her eyes, vainly trying to sleep. But sleep would not come. She knew she had only told her father half the truth. She hadn't lied – not exactly – but she felt uneasy about what she'd left out. Charlie would never forgive her if she told anyone about the lady, but she hated deceiving her father.

Kitty lay miserably in the dark, conscious of the cracking of embers in the dying fireplace, but only dimly. Her mind raced away to a dark ditch with a dead lady lying in it. Questions tumbled through her brain, each one insistent but unresolved.

Who was the lady in the ditch? Who was Mr Chamberlain? Who was Mr Peabody come to that? It was hard to know where to start. Part of her still wished that they hadn't left the body behind, but she didn't know where they would have taken it. The image of the beautiful, pale face, framed in auburn hair, floated before her eyes, as if by wishing it enough she could bring back life, and find the answers to her questions. She saw the eyes open and the lips begin to move, mouthing words she could not hear, however hard she tried. She listened, straining to hear anything, but could only make out a whisper, a murmur, still evading her understanding. She stared at the lady's lips, and finally in a rush, understanding flooded through her.

The Scarlet Ribbon.

Kitty started and opened her eyes, suddenly aware again of her surroundings. The embers had died to darkness and the room was quiet, but Kitty was alert, her every sense attentive.

The Scarlet Ribbon.

She reached into her blouse pocket and carefully pulled out the tiny, twisted material broach. This was the key. Kitty was sure of it. She had to find out what it meant - what was special about it. And now she knew where to start. It was simple. She had to ask Mr Peabody.

Chapter 3

The next morning Charlie was quiet and wouldn't quite meet her eye. As he turned his head Kitty noticed an angry red weal just above the left eyebrow. She looked at him sympathetically.

"Your Pa?"

He shook his head. Kitty didn't press the matter. She knew that other men came to live with Charlie's mother when his father was away. They never stayed very long. Kitty's mother was always scathing about it. But it wasn't Charlie's fault. He never spoke about it much, and Kitty respected that, even though she worried about him.

When they reached the Keppel's Head the curtains were still drawn. A couple of broken bottles on the steps told of the night's revelry. Kitty nervously fingered the small red ribbon in her pocket. Out in the harbour Kitty could see the dark shapes of prison hulks gradually looming out of the sea-mist, as it rolled back under the sun's warmth. She shivered slightly as she thought of all the men trapped on the hulks. She knew some of them had done terrible things, but poverty could make people desperate. Kitty knew that as well as anyone.

They didn't deserve to be doomed to the hulks. No-one deserved that.

"Well, we're here. I guess we'd better go in." Charlie nodded his agreement nervously. Kitty fought an urge to turn and walk away. Instead she climbed the couple of steps to the hotel door and rapped sharply on the knocker. For several moments nothing happened. Kitty rapped again. Eventually the door opened a small way, revealing a pair of bloodshot eyes above a waxy moustache.

"What do you want? Who are you?" The stench of stale beer followed the words. The eyes looked down at Kitty and Charlie.

"You brats better have a good reason to wake me. Or you'd better scram."

"We're here to see Mr Peabody. He told us to come."

The door shut, then opened again. This time it opened enough to see the skinny shape of a man behind the bloodshot eyes and moustache. He looked at them, still suspiciously, but with less hostility. His lips moved to reveal rotten teeth and another blast of beery breath.

"Mr Peabody eh? All right. You can come in. But stay down here while I see if he's awake. And mind you don't steal anything, eh. If you do, I'll know about it, see. So don't touch."

The man shuffled away through a door. Kitty and Charlie sat on the window sill. The reception room had three cushioned chairs and a chaise-longue, but neither of them felt comfortable to sit in them. They were unused to such luxuries, and the man had not exactly made them feel welcome.

After a short wait they heard footsteps behind the door. It opened and Kitty looked in recognition as the toff on the horse walked in, no longer adorned with the top hat, but in every other way identical.

"Well, well. If it isn't my young spy! What have you got for me young lady, and who is your friend."

Charlie felt his ears redden as the man looked at him. Kitty replied brightly,

"This is Charlie. He's helping me."

Mr Peabody ignored Charlie's diffidence, and sat beside them, smiling.

"So, young lady, what do I call you?"

"I'm Kitty. Kitty Hawkins. How do you do sir?"

She wasn't sure why she'd felt the need to add such formality, but Mr Peabody appeared amused and extended a hand to her in an equally formal fashion.

"And I am Samuel Peabody. Very pleased to make your acquaintance. Now," his voice hushed as he spoke, "what news do you have for me?"

"Well, sir, it's your lady. The one with the auburn hair. We've… we've found her."

At once his eyes sharpened.

"Yes, yes, where is she?"

Kitty choked slightly.

"She's… she's… I'm sorry sir, she's dead."

For a moment no-one moved. Then, slowly, Mr Peabody exhaled and sat back in his chair.

"Have you seen her?"

Kitty nodded.

"You're sure it's her?"

Kitty nodded again.

"How did you know it was her?"

Kitty paused.

"She was wearing this."

Kitty produced the locket that she had taken from the dead woman.

"If you look inside, it has her initials. EP. Eliza Pemberton."

Kitty opened the locket and passed it to Mr Peabody.

"She was definitely dead." she added, as if to put the matter beyond doubt.

Mr Peabody nodded seriously.

"That is sad. Very sad. But I am grateful to you both. If you don't mind, I will take this locket. It will help me in my enquiries."
Kitty did mind. For some reason, she found that she minded a lot. But she didn't feel she could really say so. She felt suddenly reluctant to show him the piece of scarlet ribbon, though still intrigued as to its meaning.
"She was clutching a ribbon as well. A scarlet ribbon. I couldn't get it out of her fingers," Kitty lied, "she was holding so tightly onto it. Does that mean anything, do you think?"
Mr Peabody paused for a moment, as if lost in thought, then answered.
"I have no idea what it might mean. It may be nothing. Where did you find her?"
"Down by the docks. In the mud. It looked like she'd washed up there."
Mr Peabody put his face in his hands.
"Do you think she drowned?"
Kitty shook her head.
"No sir, at least not by accident. She'd been sewn into a sack of hessian. Someone put her in there, and they didn't mean for her to be found."
Mr Peabody looked up, the colour draining further from his normally pallid face.

"I feared as much. And now what I so dreaded has happened. Well, I can only thank you for your assistance, tragic as the end has been."

He stood and fumbled in his jacket pocket, as if searching for a coin.

"Wait! There's more to tell you. After we found the body, there were two men. We heard them mention your name so we followed them."

"My name? They mentioned my name, you say?"

"Yes sir, and another man's name as well - a Mr Chamberlain. Do you know who he is?"

Again Mr Peabody lapsed into momentary silence before responding.

"Mr Chamberlain... Chamberlain. No I don't think I know him."

Kitty felt the hollow thud of disappointment. She had so hoped that Mr Peabody could tell them about Chamberlain, and the scarlet ribbon, but it seemed they would remain a mystery.

"So you followed them? Would you recognise them again? Where did they go?"

Kitty thought for a moment.

"I'm not really sure if I would recognise them. I mean, it was dark. Really dark. We could just about make out their shapes. I don't think I'd know their faces."

"More's the pity!" replied Mr Peabody. "Still never mind. What were you doing following them anyway?"

"They were skulking in the shadows sir. Down the back end of Penny Street. Near the prison. It did look awful suspicious sir, so me and Charlie, we just decided to follow them." The man looked impressed.

"We followed them to the Spur Redoubt and a boat came to meet them. They took someone off the boat. He was like… like a prisoner, all tied up. We followed them a little way down the seafront, but then I think… I think they saw us, so we hid."

"You are a resourceful pair. There's no doubt about it. Well done. Well done indeed. But you must realise, you have put yourselves at great risk. These are dangerous people, and they will not think twice about harming two children who get in their way."

He paused for a while, peering intently at Kitty and Charlie and interlocking his hands in front of his mouth.

"You have put yourselves in grave danger, but you are a remarkable duo. I will, of course, reward you for what you have already done, but I have more work for you, should you want it."

Kitty and Charlie glanced briefly at each other before nodding their heads eagerly.

"It is sadly too late to save Mrs Pemberton, but there is another. A son. I'd be much obliged to both you sharp-witted youngsters if you would keep an eye out for him. He's about your age, maybe slightly younger. I think twelve years. Anyway, he's vanished. I don't know where, but I expect somewhere in Portsmouth. Should you find him, there will, of course be further pecuniary recompense for your efforts."

"What's pecuniary recompense, sir?"

Charlie leaned quietly over to whisper in Kitty's ear. It was the first time he had spoken since they met Mr Peabody.

"He means there's money in it for us, Kitty."

Mr Peabody beamed and uncoiled his spider-like body from the chair, springing across the room with a sudden energy that surprised them.

"Your young friend is absolutely right. There is money in it for you. Lots of money if you succeed. But!" he stared into their eyes, suddenly fierce, "We must find him alive this time. Find the boy alive!"

Charlie looked steadily back at the man.

"Why are they all chasing him, sir? Why did they kill his mother? And who is this boy to you?"

Mr Peabody looked as if he was just about to reply, and then thought better of it. He relaxed his frantic perpetual motion and stood poised in the centre of the room. A moment later and the animation bounded back.

"Who is the boy to me? His mother was a friend of mine. I promised to look out for him if anything happened to her. Now his father has vanished and his mother is dead. As to why others are looking for him? Well, all I can tell you is that his father has been involved in some murky business, and there are some unpleasant people after the lad. So you see it is vital that I find him first."

"What is his name, this young lad, and what does he look like?"

"His name is Philip. Philip Pemberton. His hair is startlingly red, and his eyes are a bright green, like his mother's. In fact, he looks remarkably like this."

Mr Peabody flipped open Eliza's locket and Kitty and Charlie stared at the portrait of the young boy inside.

"He is older now, but still you would recognise him. He was last seen five days ago, when he and his mother alighted from a coach in Croxton Town. They paid the coach driver and tipped him handsomely. After that, neither of them was seen or heard of. Until now."

***

1819

West Africa

They had marched for days through the dust and heat, hands bound roughly in front of them, tethered to the next man in line. Lamin was used to travelling by foot, but the harshness of the march sapped his strength and his will. He saw others fall by the way side, their eyes glazing and their mouths stained with quickly drying spittle. They were cut loose and left where they fell, left for the carrion birds to feast on.
Eventually he saw the prison. He had heard stories before but never seen it. It rose from the dust, ominously impressive, its sheer stone walls filling Lamin's heart with fear.
The soldier on the gate scowled in distaste as they filed through the entrance. They were counted in and led into the yard. Shuffling from foot to foot, Lamin looked for some

chance of hope, some chance of freedom.
None came.
Crushed skin to skin with his companions he
was herded into a stone cell, lit only by a
single barred window, high and remote. The
cell was dark and airless. Crammed into the
small space, the heat and the stench were
unbearable. He felt the hot breath of the man
behind him on his neck, and the jostling of
elbows and legs as they fought for space.
Instinctively he pushed back, thinking only of
survival, still struggling to comprehend what
had happened in a few short days.

*** *** ***

They emerged, blinking in the sun, their eyes
weary with the dull morning light of the
curtained hotel.

"Extra! Extra! Read all about it! Murder
most foul ladies and gents! Murder most
foul!"

The newspaper boy's voice rang out across
the square and they hastened over to talk to
him.

"What's that you're shouting about?"

"Haven't you heard? There's been a murder.
An 'orrible murder! Found 'er this morning
they did. Dead she was. Proper dead. Police

said so."

"Who was she?"

The newspaper boy's eyes narrowed
suspiciously.

"'Ere, if you want to know so much, why
don't you buy a paper?"

Kitty smiled up at him.

"Do we look like we can afford a paper?"

The boy blushed, and looked down.

"No, suppose not. 'Ere you are then. Have a
look if you want to."

Kitty stared at the headline:

Murder most foul!

*Eliza Pemberton, lately of Chattersly House,
Somerset, was most deplorably murdered in
the small hours of the night. Her body would
not have been found, had it not been for the
brave actions of our most noble police
constable, Reginald Warren, who found the
aforementioned most wretched lady's corpse,
cast into the harbour, at three o'clock this
morning. Having no regard to his own safety,
the aforesaid Mr Warren did leap into the
said harbour and, at the expense of much
effort, and at no small risk to his own person,
did recover the body to the safety of land.*

Mrs Pemberton was the wife of George Pemberton, a gentlemen of commerce. As of yet it has not been possible to contact Mr Pemberton, whose whereabouts are unknown, however the most unfortunate lady's body has been identified by a friend of the family, namely a Mr Joseph Chamberlain.

Kitty read the article through slowly. She was better at reading than Charlie, but still it took her time. She snorted as she read of the policeman's efforts to recover the body.
" 'Brave actions!' 'Noble policeman!' We'd already done half the work for him!" she exclaimed indignantly. As she reached the end of the article she stopped and stared at the newspaper.
"Kitty? Kitty what is it?"
"Look at the name Charlie. At the end. Look at the name."
Charlie looked. Slowly he read out the word.
"Chaaam… burr… lain."
"Chamberlain. It's the name Charlie. Those men mentioned it last night. One of them said 'Mr Chamberlain'll be happy to hear of this'. What can it all mean?"
Kitty fished in her pocket and pulled out the small piece of scarlet ribbon. The newspaper boy stared at her with interest. Not much of

interest happened to him usually, and this odd girl was certainly intriguing.

"What you got there?"

"Never you mind!" Kitty retorted sharply.

The boy looked crestfallen.

"I was only asking."

Kitty relented, and gave him a thin smile.

"Ok, I'll trust you. But you mustn't breathe a word to anyone. Not anyone. If you do we'll be in big trouble."

The boy's eyes widened and he leaned forward intently.

"The lady in the story. We saw her. Last night. Dead. And she was holding this."

"Blimey! What is it?"

Before Kitty could answer she felt a tugging at her elbow. She looked round. Charlie was pulling her arm and pointing down the street. She followed his arm. At first all she could see was the bustling crowd of people, going about their daily business.

"There. Those two men. Can you see them? Are they who I think they are?"

Kitty saw them. Two men. One tall, one short. As they turned away to show their profile a wave of recognition flooded through Kitty. She would know that silhouette anywhere. She had seen it last night, brightly illuminated by a gibbous moon. They were the two men they had followed through the tunnel.

As Charlie pointed, the shorter man looked up, and stared Kitty right in the eye. He had an unsightly scar down the right side of his face, and dark whiskers adorned his cheeks. She saw no sign of recognition but the man's eyes narrowed as he saw Charlie pointing, and he tapped his colleague on the shoulder. The taller man had sallow, mildly jaundiced skin and the flesh beneath his eyes hung in loose folds. He glanced across at Kitty and Charlie and nodded. The two men started to walk slowly towards them.

"I think we'd better get out of here." whispered Charlie.

Kitty nodded. She smiled at the newspaper boy.

"Thanks for your help. Now forget you ever saw us."

They turned and started to walk away.

Behind them, Kitty could just see the two men increase their pace. They walked faster but the men were gaining on them. Instinctively, simultaneously, Kitty and Charlie both broke into a run and the men gave chase. They reached the dockyard wall and turned to run north alongside it. The men passed the

Keppel's Head and were almost at the newspaper stand.

Suddenly they heard an almighty crash.

"Oi! Watch where you're going!" came a familiar voice.

Kitty looked back. Somehow the newspaper stand had upended itself right in the path of the two men. Newspapers were scattered everywhere and the taller man lay face-down in the muck while the shorter one was struggling to his feet. The newspaper boy made a show of helping him up while haranguing the pair of them.

"That's all my days papers ruined, that is. And who's going to pay for them? You two?"

As he spoke he looked briefly up at Kitty and winked. Gratefully Kitty grabbed Charlie's hand and, without looking back again, they ran.

Chapter 4

Samuel Peabody leaned back, flexing his slender fingers against each other. They bent back at the knuckles, more than was usual. He placed the bulky pads of his thumb joints against his eyes and rubbed vigorously. He was tired.

He sat up, alert again. He couldn't afford to be tired. Too much was riding on him. He could rest later.

He thought about the girl. She was bright. No doubt about it. And inquisitive. Not a bad thing in itself. But that could get her into trouble. He would have to keep an eye out for her. Two eyes, when possible.

He paced up and down his large hotel room, the floorboards creaking slightly under his flat-footed tread. Eventually, his mind made up, he descended the stairs and sought out the beer-breathed innkeeper.

By the time he found him, the innkeeper had cleaned himself up. He had shaved and washed and his breath no longer stank so badly, although the bloodshot eyes still told the tale of the night before.

"Ah, Mr Peabody, sir. Yes sir, what can I do for you?"

"Well, you can keep an eye out for those two children for a start. If they want to see me, then you are to bring them to me immediately. Understand? Any time, day or night. And feed them next time they are here. They both look like they could use a square meal."

The innkeeper valiantly swallowed his puzzlement. Why was this fine gentleman so interested in a couple of worthless street urchins? Despite his lack of comprehension, the innkeeper had a refined sense of self-advancement, and recognised the benefit of placating this rich, and paying, customer.

"Aye sir, I'll do that, for certain I will. Either of them varmints comes knocking round here again, I'll feed 'em so full they won't need to eat for a week. Then I'll make sure I keeps 'em for you to talk to."

Mr Peabody looked at the obsequious innkeeper with ill-disguised distaste.

"Good man. See that you do."

And with that, he strode purposefully to the door, and out into the sights and sounds of Portsmouth.

***

Charlie and Kitty kept running until they were half-way down Queen Street. They didn't stop until they were sure that they were no longer pursued. Leaning back against a wall, they gasped great panting lungfuls of breath. Without quite knowing why, Kitty let out a giggle. The sudden relief of tension was overwhelming and for a few seconds they both laughed uncontrollably, hysterically. Suddenly Charlie's face was serious again.

"Do you think they recognised us? From last night, I mean."

"Don't know. One thing's for sure though. They'll recognise us again if they see us. We're going to have to watch out."

They sauntered slowly along Queen Street. Kitty noticed that she was trembling slightly. They were both sticky with sweat, that cooled quickly in the autumn breeze.

"So, where do we start?"

Charlie's brow furrowed as he wrestled with his jumbled thoughts for a few steps.

"It seems to me that we've got to find the boy first. He's the key to all this. And that's what Mr Peabody wants us to do. Problem is, we haven't got a clue where he is."

It was Kitty's turn to look thoughtful.

"Let's think about it. We have to assume he's still in the city. If he's not we'll never find him. But if he is here, then you know enough mud-larks and urchins to cover this city top to toe twice over. When was he last seen, at least as far as we know?"

"Mr Peabody said they got off the coach in Croxton Town, but we don't know exactly where."

"And we found his mother in the harbour. That narrows it down a bit, but he could have gone anywhere after that."

Charlie looked doubtful.

"I'll pass the word around. You never know, someone may have seen something. I'll have every mud-lark from here to Landport looking for him.

Kitty looked seriously at him.

"Be careful Charlie. We're not the only ones looking for him, and those two men don't strike me as pleasant company for anyone. Besides, we don't know who else they may be working with."

Charlie nodded his head eagerly.

"Don't worry about me Kitty. You need to be careful too. What are you going to do?"

Kitty looked determined.

"I'm going to find out about this Mr Chamberlain. He's cropped up too many times to be coincidence. I know he's involved in this and I mean to find out how."

Again Charlie looked doubtful.

"How do you plan to find him?"

Kitty smiled mischievously.

"I'm going to sell candles."

***

Mr Joseph Chamberlain sat in the darkest corner of the alehouse and regarded his fingernails. The alehouse was quiet, almost empty, most of its custom saving itself for the evening revelries. Absent-mindedly he picked at a small piece of dirt, trapped beneath the nail of his left ring finger. The finger held no ring, but a pale line indicated that there had recently been one present. His left hand travelled surreptitiously up to his lapel and felt carefully behind it. He felt the smooth twists of the ribbon against his fingers, and the tiny pin that held it in place. Mr Chamberlain pulled out his pewter pocket watch and flipped open the lid. If the watch was correct it was seven minutes past the hour. He sipped his beer and tutted in mild annoyance. A serving girl approached with a flagon of ale and looked towards him enquiringly. He waved her away. He needed all his wits about him at the moment. Eventually the door opened and he saw them enter. They looked around, eyes staring into the dim light of the tavern. He made no signal, but eventually the short one spotted him and pointed him out to his companion. They threaded their way through the closely packed chairs and tables to where he sat.

"You're late."

He did not look up but motioned to them to sit down.

"Sorry Mr Chamberlain, I'm sure, but we had good reason."

"Really? What might that be?"

"We saw the two children. The ones as must have spotted us last night."

"Ah, yes, how careless of you. Your negligence has left us in a distinctly awkward situation. You do realise, don't you, that the police will have to look into this now. You are aware, I take it, that they have found her body?"

The two men looked down into their beer and said nothing. Chamberlain chuckled inwardly at their obvious resentment. But they dared not say anything. At length, Chamberlain broke the silence.

"What do you plan to do next?"

The taller of the men smiled conspiratorially. At least it was supposed to be conspiratorial, but it came out as more of a lop-sided sneer.

"Don't worry Mr Chamberlain. We'll find the children. They won't be able to hide from us for long."

***

Kitty slung the bag of candles around her shoulder to hang at her waist. She adjusted her shawl and smoothed down the rough cotton of her dress. It was faded and patched in many places, but it was her best dress. In fact it was her only proper dress. Her mother had been given it by another mother whose daughter had died. Despite the sadness, her mother was pragmatic about these things. You didn't waste a good dress.
Kitty did not usually take much trouble with her appearance.
"If you made yourself up better, you'd sell more candles!" her mother often grumbled. But today her mother had no cause for complaint. Kitty was making herself up with painstaking care and attention to detail. The additional effort was not purely for the sake of increased profit. The two men were looking for an urchin in rags, that could have passed for a boy or a girl. Hopefully they would not see the young girl selling candles as she passed beneath their noses.

By the time she was ready the streets were thronging with sellers, peddling everything from moustache wax to… well, candles. She joined in, allowing the flow of people to enfold her and carry her along. All around her the street-sellers shouted lustily to advertise their wares. Kitty kept quiet. She usually did. People would always need candles.

***

Joseph Chamberlain let the tavern door swing shut behind him as he stepped out into the kaleidoscope of activity that was Spice Island. It was still early in the day but that didn't stop the revelry. If you wanted to find a den of drunken iniquity, then this was the place to come. A couple of sailors were lying asleep by the camber dock, their pockets long since picked by the enterprising youth of Portsea. The sun had burnt off the haze and the sailors' bare upper bodies were reddening quickly in the heat. He could smell their unwashed sweat from ten feet away. He sniffed in distaste, and then smiled to himself. They would have a terrible headache when they woke.

Joseph Chamberlain often found humanity distasteful. He was not given to an overly sentimental view of life, and rather considered that the purpose of other people was to facilitate his clandestine designs. Unfortunately this necessitated liaison with some of the less desirable elements of humanity, most of whom could be found in Spice Island.

He was crossing towards the large chandlery building on the other side of the road when he noticed a nondescript character in a dark coat detach himself from a particularly noisome group of sailors. The man did not look at him, nor appear to be deliberately heading towards him. Nonetheless their paths converged and the two men fell into step side by side. Joseph spoke without looking at his companion.

"They have lost the boy, and the woman has been found. Dead, at least, but nonetheless, things have not gone to plan."

The man nodded his head in agreement.

"Things have not gone to plan," he echoed, "but she will not talk, and the boy will be found."

"There is another… complication. A young girl, Kitty Hawkins. She has seen too much. I trust you to take care of things, my friend."

"I believe our esteemed colleagues are already looking into this Mr Chamberlain."

Joseph Chamberlain gave a sidelong glance at his associate.

"Yes, indeed they are, Mr Moseley. And you will keep your eyes on them, lest they… fall short again. Such an event will, of course, be your responsibility."

The man smiled. The grin split his pockmarked face uninvitingly.

"Naturally Mr Chamberlain. Naturally"

And as naturally as the two men had come together, their paths diverged and they went their separate ways.

***

Kitty made her way inland through the town, away from the heaving masses of people in Portsea. She headed for the terraces. Eliza Pemberton had last been seen in that part of town, and besides, there was more money to be made selling to the rich houses than hawking her wares on the poorer streets. It was odd giving the lady a name. It made her seem more real. She had seemed real enough when they pulled her out of the mud. Her mind flashed back, unbidden to that moment, recreating every detail of her beautiful, pallid face, streaked in mud and framed in a mane of auburn curls. She felt almost as if she'd known her, so strong was the emotion. Kitty shook herself gently. No sense indulging in fanciful thoughts like that! She'd be better off concentrating on the here and now. And the here was King's Terrace, and the now was a late Tuesday morning in 1831. Kitty approached the first house in the terrace. The houses were new, and swept in grand facades away from the road. Stone steps led up to the front door, ornately adorned with brass plaque and knocker. Clutching up her skirts and her courage she ascended the steps and knocked nervously.

After a long pause the door opened, though not fully. A wary and wizened face peered out, framed by a black bonnet above a black dress. The sharp eyes seemed to look right through Kitty. The head nodded towards the side of the house.

"Round the back."

The door shut and Kitty was left on the step. Kitty made her way to the corner and along the backs of the terraces, where tradespeople were received. She was not upset at her lack of welcome. She had expected it. But this way, hopefully someone would be waiting for her at the back door, not leave her sitting on the step.

Sure enough, there was a young woman waiting to meet her. She had clearly been warned what Kitty was selling.

"Candles? Well with winter coming we could always use more. I'll ask the housekeeper. She may see fit to buy some."

The young woman disappeared and returned a short while later with the rather austere lady in the black bonnet.

"Ah, it's you again girl. In future it would be much appreciated if you arrived at the appropriate entrance. That is to say, the rear entrance."

She sounded like she had practised hard to develop an air of superiority that didn't quite come naturally. Still, thought Kitty, no sense in upsetting my first customer. At least not any more than I already have.

"Candles?" she ventured, proffering the said objects.

The housekeeper looked at them and sniffed. "Hmm. Tallow. Cheap but well made."

She said the word 'cheap' with a slight emphasis, as if daring Kitty to say otherwise. Instead, Kitty opted for the direct approach. "Sixpence a bundle ma'am."

Again the housekeeper sniffed.

"Hmm. I'll give you sixpence for two bundles. That's my final offer."

Kitty sensed that there was nothing further to be gained and reluctantly agreed. The housekeeper sniffed once more, a polished and practiced nasal sound which was as much of a dismissal as any words could convey. She turned her back and stalked back into the house, leaving Kitty and the younger maid staring at her.

"Sorry about her. She's always like that." said the young maid. Kitty made a mock grimace and shrugged her shoulders carelessly.

"I'll get your money, just wait here a moment."

The maid disappeared for a few seconds and returned with sixpence, brandished carefully in front of her. She dropped the coin in Kitty's upturned palm, business finished, but unsure if there was anything left to say. Kitty seized her chance.

"Thank you. And don't worry about *her*. I wonder if you can help me though. I'm looking for a Mr Chamberlain. Do you know him?"

The maid stared blankly.

"Mr Chamberlain? No, never heard of him. It's Mr Addison as runs this house. Do you

want me to tell him you called?"
"No, don't worry. Thank you anyway."
It had been a long shot, but Kitty couldn't
help feeling a slight pang of disappointment.

***

By the end of the morning Kitty had been to
thirteen houses. She had sold seven of her
bundles of candles, received four polite
refusals, and had two doors shut in her face.
No-one had heard of Mr Chamberlain. Kitty
was not deterred by her lack of success. After
her initial disappointment she had come to
accept that the chances were small. Still, she
reasoned, if you took lots of small chances
and put them together, surely that was similar
to making one much larger chance?
She wondered how Charlie was getting on.
Kitty thought slightly wistfully about Charlie,
covered in mud, digging for treasure, while
she, combed and bonneted, made polite
conversation with the maids of fashionable
society. She knew that she *ought* to be more
ladylike (as her mother quite often reminded
her). But then there were many other things
that she *ought* to be and she couldn't manage
all of them. If she asked her mother, for
instance, she probably *ought not* to be

searching for a gentleman that she did not know, and whose only connection to her was that he knew a murdered woman that she had found. Kitty smiled briefly at the thought of her mother's face if only she knew. Then she frowned and put the thought away. She would not wish that on her mother.

She had no jealousy as she saw inside the fine houses of the terraces. They were grand. Far grander than any building Kitty had ever stepped into, other than a church. But when she saw the staid and starched lives of the maidservants and house-keepers who greeted her, she felt only a sense of entrapment and an overwhelming urge to run away.

It was at the fifteenth house that fortune finally started to look more kindly upon her. As with all the other houses, she found her way to the back of the house where trades-people and artisans would be received. On this occasion it was a young man who answered the door. He was a burly figure, whose arms didn't quite seem to fit in the sleeves of his jacket. Instead of the clipped and carefully polished articulations of the maidservants, he spoke with the rougher twang of Portsmouth, occasionally catching himself mid-way through a sentence to flatten his vowels and sharpen his consonants.

"Yeah? What do you want? Ah, you selling candles?"

It seemed that news did not travel that fast in the terraces. Kitty smiled. Where she lived there would be no such opportunity for anonymity. If anything happened, everyone knew about it pretty fast.

Still grateful for the lack of recognition, she persevered.

"Hello," she replied, they're sixpence a pack. The young man shook his head.

"I don't think she will take that. Not sixpence. We can probably get them cheaper in town."

Kitty opened her mouth to argue, then thought better of it. She turned to leave, but the man stopped her.

"Here, don't I know you?"

Kitty shook her head, slightly confusedly. She didn't think she knew him. But then there were any number of places he might have recognised her from.

"Yes I do. You're Kitty aren't you? Mr Pounds teaches you. He used to teach me too. My name's Frank. Frank Stourton. He still teaches my sister, Mary."

Kitty did remember. She knew Mary Stourton, and she had a vague recollection of her older brother, but he had gone away a few years' back – to work in the King's Terrace house Kitty supposed. He hadn't been as big back then. Tall but not so broad.

"Yes, of course, Frank. How nice to see you."

The man smiled.

"Tell you what Kitty, give us a packet. Here's sixpence for you, and I'll see if I can talk her ladyship round to paying me back."

Kitty accepted the sixpence gratefully, and seeing it as a conversational opening thought she might push her luck a little further.

"Frank, I don't know if you can help me with something else. I'm looking for a Mr Chamberlain. I don't know if you know him?"

Frank's eyes narrowed.

"Mr Chamberlain. Why are you looking for him?"

Kitty sighed.

"It's a bit complicated." She looked down demurely, or as close to demurely as she could muster. "He helped me once, and I wanted to thank him."

It wasn't a great lie, but it was the best she could come up with on the spot. Frank didn't appear to question it.

"I don't know Mr Chamberlain Kitty, but you're the second person today who's mentioned the name."

Kitty looked up in surprise.

"The police came past here this morning. They weren't looking for Mr Chamberlain, they were looking for a boy. Some Philip Pemberton. Not that I'd ever heard of him at all. Probably run away from the workhouse for all I know. Anyway, I told them I couldn't help them, and they went away. It was just as they were leaving and one of them said to the other, he said, 'Mr Chamberlain won't like this you know. Not one bit of it.' Anyway, I didn't have a clue what they were on about so I paid it no mind, but then a couple of hours later and there's you on the doorstep asking about the very same gentleman. Sounds a bit fishy to me."

He attempted to fix her with a piercing gaze, but from his broad and cheerful face, it looked more startled than piercing. Nonetheless Kitty felt a slight shiver as she asked,

"And can you remember what they looked like, these policemen."

"Of course I can. Funny fellows they were. One tall and skinny as a bean. The other short and round as a ball." His eyes narrowed again. "Why? What's it to you?"

"No matter, just curious," replied Kitty, far more airily than she felt, "and thanks for buying the candles."

***

1820

Atlantic Ocean

Rain lashed through the slatted cargo hatch above them, stinging the skin without mercy. In the darkness a man's voice moaned – whether in fear or pain Lamin did not know. The ship lurched again, causing another well of nausea to rise up within him. Lamin bit the inside of his mouth and tasted the salt of blood. He mustn't throw up. He couldn't afford to lose the strength.
He could hear retching all around him. The stench of vomit filled the air. The moans grew fainter, softening to whimpers, before they died out altogether. Lamin closed his eyes and prayed for the man. The sailors would try to keep them alive. They guarded their precious cargo jealously. But the storm was all consuming. Lamin and his companions were forgotten, ignored in the desperate fight for the ship's survival.

He closed his eyes tighter, feeling the pressure build in his skull. If he tried hard he could take himself away, take himself back to Africa. But that brought no relief either. Just the sound of his wife's screams as he was torn from her, torn from his children, torn from his home.

He saw once more the look in his enemy's eyes as he was rounded up and sold for the promise of guns and bullets. He felt once again the crack of the whip that cowed them into submission, and the humiliation as he stood, naked and bound, in the slave-market, pushed and prodded by traders who examined him as they might a rare fruit. He saw once more the contempt of the white man who threw him into the filthiest bowel of the ship, he and his countrymen, herded like animals. No, he reminded himself. They treated their animals with more respect. And again he heard, echoing within his mind, the screams of his children, and the crying of his baby as she heard her mother sobbing.

Lamin opened his eyes. He could endure the pain better than he could the screams. He would stay here, in this wretched hold, tossed between storm and wave, and he would survive.

***

"Kitty! Kitty Hawkins!"

Kitty started at her name and looked around to see where it came from. As she turned, two bundles of candles escaped from her bag and spilled themselves across the cobbled street. The tall ungainly boy that stooped to help her looked familiar, but for a moment Kitty struggled to place him. He deftly gathered up the scattered candles that rolled in the dirt and smiled up at her, part cheeky, part nervous. As he smiled recognition dawned.

"You're the newspaper seller, aren't you?"

"That's me. 'Extra! Extra! Read all about it!'"

"How did you know my name? I don't think I told you."

"Ah, well, I know people everywhere, I do. Information is my business you see."

Kitty was not going to let him off that easily. She glowered at him.

"I thought I told you to forget you'd ever seen us."

"I did forget. I forgot completely. I forgot so much that a certain two gentlemen were really quite agitated. And then I heard your name on the street and I remembered again."

Kitty was slightly mollified.

"Look, I should have thanked you before. You really helped us out this morning, and you don't even know me. You didn't need to do that. So… thanks."

Kitty paused, unsure what else to say. 'Thanks' seemed just a little inadequate, so she flashed a smile at the boy. He smiled back.

"That's all right. You looked like you needed a hand. Besides, it's not my fault if people don't look where they're going. I can't help it if two idiots crash into my newspaper stand."

He winked at Kitty and held a hand out to her.

"I'm Ned. Ned Parsons."

Kitty shook the hand.

"Now then Kitty, the word is that you're looking for someone. I ain't promising, but let's just say I might be able to help you."

Kitty tried to hide her eagerness.

"Do you know something about him then?"

"Like I said, information's my business. Nothing happens without me knowing."

He puffed his chest out, slightly self-importantly Kitty thought.

"If you come to the Flathouse Rookery at dusk today you might see something that's of interest to you."

"Will Philip be there? Have you seen him?"

But Ned refused to be drawn further.

"This evening. Meet at Unicorn Gate. Seven o'clock sharp. Ask for Polly. That's all I'm saying for now. Oh… and…good luck!" Ned turned and walked back towards the docks, whistling cheerfully to himself. Kitty watched him go, her thoughts churning. She needed to find Charlie, and quickly. It had been a most eventful day already, but she had a feeling there was more to come before the day was over.

Chapter 5

A visitor to Portsmouth, approaching the splendour of Unicorn Gate, would have been forgiven for ignoring the sight of Flathouse Rookery to their north. The rookery was a twisted maze of half-repaired derelict buildings and wooden shacks, squeezed between the docks and the new houses of Landport. The buildings, such as they were, leaned precariously against each other, as they stretched west towards the mudflats of the harbour. Here the streets gave way to a maze of slick, muddy tracks which ran with sewage when it rained. The tracks were overrun with rats, and raised wooden walkways linked many of the buildings.

Charlie waited nervously at the edge of the rookery, watching the sun set behind the silhouetted buildings, casting pencil thin beams of redness across Portsmouth harbour. He wondered, not for the first time, if they had been wise to come. It was not an area he would normally have ventured into, and Charlie would cheerfully venture into most places. It was even less an area that he would want to bring Kitty, although Kitty, he had to admit, showed no such qualms, and was calmly surveying the scene as if they had come purely for the pleasure of the view. Charlie's trepidation was not tested for long. Within minutes of their arrival they heard a low whistle coming from just behind them. They were both slightly startled as they had not noticed anyone else around, but seconds later a girl appeared, a bit older than Kitty and Charlie but not much. The girl was dirty. Far dirtier than Charlie or Kitty, although, Kitty reminded herself, they would have been closely matched the night before. And she was ragged. Charlie and Kitty may have been shabby, with their patched and handed-down clothes, but this girl was positively ragged. Her clothes were little more than strips of material loosely held together, and would hardly provide much protection from the coming winter. Her hair was (as far as Kitty could tell) a dark brown, and appeared tangled and matted. She was, in Kitty's initial estimation, dirty and ragged.

She was also agile. She swung herself down lithely from one of the raised wooden walkways to stand defiantly before them.

"Are you Polly?"

The girl ignored Kitty's question.

"Word is you're lookin' for a boy."

"Yes," replied Kitty, "a Philip Pemberton. Have you seen him?"

"Maybe I have, maybe I ain't. Depends on who wants to know. And why."

She stared at the two of them, as if daring them to challenge her. Kitty decided that honesty would be as sound a policy as any other.

"I'm Kitty, and this is Charlie. We found his mother. Well her corpse anyway. In the harbour."

The girl's eyes widened in astonishment.

"That was you, was it? I thought it was the beak. Still that don't tell me what you want with Philip."

"So you have seen him then?"

"Sharp ain't yer. Yes, I've seen him. But I ain't taking you to him unless you tell me what you want."

Kitty felt she could easily get into a stalemate against this fiercely stubborn protector of Philip's.

"Look, we don't know Philip, but we know he's in danger. We weren't the only ones looking for his mother. There's a Mr Chamberlain as well – we don't know how he's connected to this but he is. And he's got the police on his side. They've been chasing us too. We've got to find Philip before they do."

Where the girl had been wavering in her opinion, it appeared that this last revelation decided her.

"Police chasin' you are they? Well, I guess in that case I can trust you. Don't let me down, mind. I knows everyone in this town. I can always find you again."

She said this last sentence with a note of warmth that disarmed the threat in the words.

"Come on then. Follow me."

The girl turned to go. Kitty followed her. Charlie wavered for a moment and then called out.

"Wait! What's your name?"

"Polly. Polly Perkins. And who said you could come? I only meant the girl."

This threw Charlie into a state of bewilderment.

"B-but I, I need to c-come. Need to b-be with Kitty."

He looked at Kitty and his face reddened. Polly Perkins smirked, then threw back her head and roared with laughter.

"Ha! Don't you worry my young lover. I was only pulling your leg. You can come too. Now let's go before the beak are following you again."

They threaded their way through the narrow alleys and up over the timber gangways that linked so many of the buildings. Kitty looked out around her. Mostly she could see just the daily smog of the town, but every now and then the cloying cloud parted and she caught a glimpse of the harbour spreading out beneath her, the sea fading dull green into the backdrop of the country beyond.

It didn't take long for Kitty to lose her sense of direction. She was impressed by Polly's sure-footedness and attempted to emulate the older girl's confidence. Occasionally, however, she slipped on a muddy board and had to catch herself before she fell. On one occasion Charlie shot an arm out and caught her. She glowered at him ungratefully.

"I'm ok. You didn't need to do that."

He shrugged his shoulders and let go of her arm. Kitty felt a momentary sense of remorse, before the excitement returned. Eventually, after many twists, turns, ascendings and descendings, and more than one near-fatal slip, they reached an old wooden building, equally dilapidated and ramshackle as its neighbours. As they approached it, a whistle came from a window way above them. Kitty and Charlie looked up and for a moment saw a lad, about their own age, sat in the window, before he disappeared from view. An answering whistle sounded from inside the building and a makeshift brown curtain of sackcloth was pulled fractionally to one side. A grubby face peered out.

"All right Polly?" he said. "Who are your friends?"

"They've come to see Philip."

"Oh they have, have they?" The voice assumed a poorly imitated air of poshness. "Well step this way my lords and ladies. Do come in?"

Polly grinned.

"Give over, Flynn. They're all right. Besides, they've got the beak on their tail."

"Well why didn't you say so!"

The brown curtain was pulled quickly back and they saw that the grubby face belonged to an equally grubby, raggedly dressed boy who grinned to show as many gaps as there were teeth.

"Quickly then folks! Don't hang about, else the beak'll be onto all of us."

He ushered them through the doorway into the dingiest, dankest room that Kitty had ever seen. Kitty considered herself well-versed in the rougher elements of society, yet she had never seen anywhere as depressingly dirty as this.

The room was long and thin, like an extremely wide corridor. Along each side lay a string of what could very loosely be termed beds. Except they weren't beds. They were more collections of rugs, old clothes, rags, and anything that could be roughly fashioned into a mattress. On some of the beds lay sleeping boys and girls, of various ages, some of them lying atop the bedding, others barely visible lumps within the massed piles of material.

"Welcome to our humble abode." Flynn bowed, partly in mock courtesy, partly out of necessity, as he ducked beneath a low beam. Without warning he raised his voice to a harsh bellow.

"Philip! Your friends are here!"

He grinned at Polly. Half way down the opposite side of the wall a lump under a pile of rags moved. A face stared out. It was a surprisingly clean face, at least in comparison to those all around. And notably it still had all its teeth. It was also a scared face, although it was doing its best to smile valiantly. It looked nervously at Kitty and Charlie.

"Hello," it said, "I'm Philip."

***

Philip looked from one face to another and unconsciously licked his lips. He looked starving. All the children looked hungry, but Philip looked less accustomed to the experience than the other children. Kitty had been hungry before. She remembered that feeling of hunger gnawing at your innards, eating you from the inside out. She shuddered briefly at the recollection. She didn't want to go back there, but the children were taking her.

Philip was different though. He was not fat, but neither was he scrawny like his under-nourished companions. His clothes were dirty with fresh dirt, but well-made and surprisingly un-tattered. His mop of blond hair had been recently cut. The edges were neatly trimmed, even if it hadn't been brushed for a few days.

Charlie smiled encouragingly at him. Unfortunately the effect was somewhat marred by the large gap where his tooth should have been, but Philip seemed to warm to his cheerfulness.

"Look, Philip, I know you don't know us, but you need to trust us. We're here to help you."

Philip looked up, disarmingly trusting, given his circumstances.

"How will you help me?"

Charlie stopped. He hadn't thought that far ahead. How could they help him? They could hardly go to the police, and it occurred to him that they weren't in much better a situation themselves than young Philip. He looked at Kitty. She was not quite avoiding his gaze but still didn't directly meet his eye. Neither seemed to know how to say what they had to tell the boy.

Eventually Charlie cleared his throat.

"Philip, I'm sorry, it's about your mother…"

"She's dead. I know."

Charlie was caught by surprise. On reflection, the news had been plastered all over the papers, but still he hadn't expected Philip to be so forthright. He nodded.

"Yes. She's dead I'm afraid. We found her body, in the mud, last night."

He grimaced at the recollection, and it occurred to him that he may have given more detail than necessary.

"She was attacked. We don't know who by, but we saw the two men who put her in the moat. It might have been them."

This time the boy nodded, and Charlie saw the tiniest flicker of fear flash across his face, before being replaced by a mask of expressionless numbness.

"It was them. They attacked both of us."
This time it was Kitty who spoke, softly but insistently.

"What happened Philip?"
The boy looked at her and there was a slight melting of the mask.

"We were walking. I don't really know where we were. But they were waiting for us. They came out of the shadows and… and…"
The boy broke off, gulping heavily. Kitty and Charlie looked away, allowing him time to compose himself. After a few more moments he looked up. This time he stared directly into Kitty's face, his eyes tear-stained but unwavering.

"I ran away. I ran and left her. And that's the last time I ever saw her."
Again he broke off and turned away. Kitty walked over to him and placed an arm around his shoulder. He didn't move.

"If you'd stayed you'd be dead as well."
Polly's voice came from across the room.

"After what they did, they'd never have let you live. You were lucky we found you when we did."
Polly looked up at Kitty and Charlie.

"We found him a few streets away from the

workhouse, just wandering around. It was obvious he didn't belong on the street and we felt sorry for him. Besides, he looked like he was worth a penny or two and we didn't want someone else cutting his throat for his money."

Her tone was friendly but Charlie couldn't help the nagging thought that they may have wanted to do that for themselves.

"We brought him back here and he's been with us ever since. But he don't belong here, bless him."

Kitty looked across at Philip.

"Does the name Peabody mean anything to you?"

Philip shook his head disconsolately.

"I don't think I've ever heard of him. I mean, is it a he? Is it a man or a woman?"

"A man. Tall and thin, with a beard and a monocle. He's asked us to watch out for you. Says he knew your mother."

"I can't say for sure. Maybe he did know my mother. But I don't remember him at all."

Kitty tried another tack. She pulled the piece of scarlet ribbon out of her pocket.

"What about this. Do you recognise this?"

Philip's eyes widened.

"Yes. Of course. It's the scarlet ribbon. My father's scarlet ribbon."

"I took it from the body of your mother when we found her. To stop her enemies from finding it. It wasn't hers though, you say."

"No, it was my father's. I don't know why my mother would have been wearing it."

Philip gave a wry smile and then a gulp.

"I never talked about it with my mother. My father always said it was a secret."

Do you know what it is? What it means?

Philip looked uncomfortable, as if he knew something but was not sure whether to tell them. He shifted his weight from one side to another for a few seconds, and his eyes slid down to the left. Then he seemed to make his mind up and his eyes caught Kitty's again.

"It's the sign of the Scarlet Order. It's a secret order. My father's secret order."

Kitty and Charlie were startled. Of all the possible responses, they had not expected this. Charlie butted in excitedly.

"A secret order! And what does it do, this Scarlet Order?"

Philip looked deflated.

"I don't really know. I mean, my father wouldn't tell me much about it. After all, it was supposed to be secret. I asked him about the ribbon once and he said it was a special sign. Everyone in the order wore it when they met."

Kitty hid her frustration. They were, she reminded herself, a long way further than they had been at the beginning of the day. At least a few more pieces of the puzzle had fallen into place. She scratched her head, absent-mindedly, and as she did so another thought came to her.

"And what about Mr Chamberlain? Does that name mean anything to you?"

The transformation was startling. A moment before, the boy had been nervous but composed. Now naked fear was written across Philip's face.

"He was in the order. My father's order. I never saw him, but I remember my father telling my mother about him."

"And what did your father say about him, about Mr Chamberlain?"

"He was scared of him. My father wasn't scared of anyone, but he was scared of Mr Chamberlain. He used to say he was the devil, and that if anything ever happened to him, then it would be the devil's work."

**

The man lay in the dark, shackled and shivering. He was cold, so cold. The hunger he could bear. He had been hungry many times in his life. But the cold was all-pervading, creeping into his bones like the icy fingers of death. He closed his eyes, straining desperately to recall the heat of his homeland, but its warmth was ever more elusive, and his consciousness returned unwillingly to the dank and frozen misery of his cell.

He did not know how long he had been here. One or two days, he thought, but time had long ceased to be meaningful. In his solitary confinement, he drifted in and out of consciousness, woken by the rats, nibbling cautiously at his feet. They were so far too timid to risk more than an exploratory nuzzle, but it was only a matter of meaningless time before their hunger overcame their fear.

He wondered what had become of his wife, his children. Were they safe? Had they escaped? Or did they, too, lie dripping and bleeding in some god-forsaken hole as he did. He prayed for them, forcing his mind to see them, as they had been, another world away. Opening his eyes, the familiar blackness rushed in on him once more. The silence was broken only by the dripping of water and the rustle of the rats. He strained his eyes into the gloom, but to no avail.

The man became aware of a shuffling noise from beyond the cell. He recognised the ungainly tread, and anticipated the scratching of the key in the lock. He laughed, humourlessly. How dangerous did they think he was? Chained and manacled, still they locked him within his cell. What were they expecting - miracles?

The cell door creaked slowly open. The shaft of dull grey light from the tunnel beyond was almost dazzling in its contrast to the seemingly endless dark. He heard the harsh rasp of his captors' voice.

"Here you are my fine gentleman. Ha!" The voice barked out a staccato laugh. "We can't have you dying on us now, can we?"

In the gloom he could just make out an arm, placing a plate and a cup of water by his side. He stayed still and silent.

"Ungrateful swine!" A hand cuffed him around the head, hard enough to hurt but not to harm. "Think yourself lucky I feed you at all."

The shuffling tread faded away from him and gradually the cell door creaked shut.

Chapter 6

Mr Joseph Chamberlain rested back in his chair and cracked his knuckles satisfyingly. He looked thoughtfully at the pieces before him, the familiar shapes silhouetted against the black and white squares of the board. Slowly but purposefully he pushed a pawn one place forward into the path of the opposing queen. The pawn would be taken of course. It did not matter. In the long run it had served its purpose. Sometimes one had to make such sacrifices to win the game. He looked up and smiled at the man opposite him.

"Your move I believe."

His opponent said nothing. Nor did he return Mr Chamberlain's smile. His face, Mr Chamberlain reflected, did not look like one accustomed to smiling. In contrast to the smooth skin and neatly clipped beard of Mr Chamberlain, the face of his adversary was pockmarked and roughened, with patchy stubble pushing out between angry red crevices. It was a face that had seen the summers and winters come and go, and worn the worst of both.

Eventually the man took his pawn. Mr Chamberlain worked hard to keep the glee from his face, smiling inwardly at the naivety. He sipped slowly at the glass of wine in his hand. Its bitterness burned his mouth. It was rough, and Mr Chamberlain was used to the finer things in life. But it was the best they had, and Mr Chamberlain was also used to making the best of things. He moved his Knight, three squares forward and one to the side.

"They will find him, you know. The boy. They will find him. The only question is whether he will still be alive."

"He had better be, for their sake." Mr Chamberlain's smile was particularly ingratiating, as if to lessen the threat of the words. "He is the only link we have."

The man opposite swallowed and moved his queen to take Mr Chamberlain's Bishop. Again Mr Chamberlain smiled to himself. It was all so predictable.

"In any case, Mr Moseley, I will trust you to take care of our… ah… compatriots. All in due course, of course."

Mr Moseley swallowed again and stared down at the chess board. Mr Chamberlain moved his Knight once more.

"Check."

The man had no choice. He had to move his king out of the way. Remove all their options and you knew what they would do. It was always the way. He moved his Rook and smiled once more across the table.

"Check mate."

***

Rain pounded against the roofs and thudded into gutters as Kitty and Charlie made their way to Mr Pounds' school. In the streets, the rainwater mixed with the soil, and the cobbles were quickly covered with a thick, pungent slurry. Philip looked around him, wide-eyed, as they ran. The rain had soaked into his clothes and he was colder and more uncomfortable than he was used to being. Nonetheless he did not complain. He had learnt to value any human kindness in the last few days, and he trusted that Kitty and Charlie meant him no harm.

Mr Pounds showed no surprise at Philip's presence. Children came and went at his school, and all were welcome who chose to attend. The old man found a stale crust of bread to offer the boy, and noted how eagerly he devoured it. It was clear that the boy had a story, but equally clear that he did not wish to share it. He watched the initial wariness in the boy's eyes give way to enthusiasm as he relaxed into the lesson. He was clearly well-educated, and as he answered questions in clear, and increasingly confident, tones the other children looked on in surprise, some in respect and others in envy.

Mr Pounds did not know how Kitty and Charlie had come across the boy, and they wouldn't tell him. They were quietly protective, fending off any intrusive questions the other children addressed to Philip, and moving the topic of conversation on quickly if it strayed too close to Philip's background. Towards the end of the morning's lessons he found some time to talk to them, away from the other children.

"Is there anything you wish to tell me?"

The children looked evasively at each other. For a moment they said nothing. Then Kitty asked,

"Do you know anything about the Scarlet Order Mr Pounds?"

He thought for a moment and shook his head.

"Never heard of it. Why do you ask."

"Oh, no matter. We're trying to find out more about it. It's a society. A secret society."

Mr Pounds chuckled.

"Well I guess that's why I've never heard of it then."

He looked at their solemn faces and his laughter dried in his mouth.

"Sorry children, I can't help you on this occasion, but if I find anything out I'll be sure to let you know." he added brightly.

By the time they left the cobbler's shop, the rain had slowed to a steady drizzle. The streets were still awash, but the going was easier without the rivulets flowing down their collars and under their clothes. As they passed the workhouse Philip's nervousness returned. Kitty looked at him sympathetically.

"I know, Philip, some bad things happened here. But they won't happen again. You're with us now."

He smiled up at her gratefully, and for a moment his face opened in trust. A second later the fear returned and his eyes rounded in anxiety. He started to gesture but Charlie had already seen the danger and pulled him into the shelter of a narrow brick archway. On the other side of the road, just visible in the distance were two familiar figures, one tall and thin, one short and squat. Their previous pursuers had not yet seen them, and Kitty dived under the arch after Charlie and Philip, out of view just in time. Philip was shaking violently. He didn't speak, but shrank to the back of the archway.

"Was that them? The ones who killed your mother?"

He nodded silently.

"Don't worry Philip. We won't let them take you. We'll find somewhere safe for you."

Kitty wished she felt as confident as she sounded. The boy's trusting look was almost too much to bear.

"We've got to get him off the street. He's not safe here. They'll find him soon enough. Where shall we take him, Kitty?"

Kitty knew that Charlie was right. He wasn't safe on the street. She thought for a moment, but the answer was obvious.

"Peabody. Let's take him to Peabody."

Charlie nodded, but uncertainly.

"Are you sure we can trust him? I mean, we don't actually know him."

"I know Charlie, but he knew Philip's mother, and he tried to help her. Besides, he's the only option we've got."

***

1826

Jamaica

It was late afternoon and the Caribbean sun was low, casting long shadows through the plantation. Jacob's hands were rough and sticky with sap. He straightened slowly and stretched his aching back, feeling the knots ripple down the sides of his spine. The air felt dense and heavy, weighed down by the sweetness of the sugar cane, and undisturbed by any breeze on such a clear, windless day. In the background he could hear the hum of the harvesters' machetes, and the low tones of singing from his fellow slaves. Above their constant chorus he heard the harsher shouts of the white man he called his master. Jacob bit back the words before they caught in his throat.

The white man was coming closer. The voice grew louder. He could hear the stamp of the man's boots on the hard soil. The bushes parted in front of him and he looked into the pink, sun-scorched face.

"Jacob."

"Yes master?"

"I have a job for you. Go and get cleaned up and then bring the trap round to the front of

the house. I need to go into town and I want you to drive me."

"Yes master."

Jacob made his way to the wooden shack in which he slept. He fetched himself a bowl and gave himself a quick wash. It was too cursory to cleanse the sticky sweat from his long hours of toil, but he felt better for it, and gratefully changed his clothes, enjoying the feel of clean cotton against his skin. He had found himself increasingly the object of his master's attention recently. It seemed that, if ever a job needed to be done, he would be the chosen one. Whether it was to fix some item of domestic importance in the big house, to take his master into town, or to run some trivial errand for his master's children, it was always Jacob that his master sought.

He led the horse from the stable. She was a small white mare, sometimes skittish, but today docile under his gentle touch. She waited patiently while he hitched her up to the trap, and trotted obediently as he directed her with the reins. Jacob smiled ruefully at her unquestioning obedience. Were they so dissimilar, he and the horse?

At the front of the house his master was remonstrating playfully with two of his children.

"What shall I bring you? Why should I bring you anything? Yes, I know I am going into town, but why should that mean gifts?"

The children squeaked and giggled, hopefully, not believing the miserly words for a moment. The master ruffled their heads briefly and strode over to where Jacob stood, holding the horse's head while he softly whispered into her ear.

"You drive Jacob, I'll sit alongside you. We have some stores to collect but I want us to be back before dark."

"Yes master."

They rode for a while in silence, just the rattle of the trap and the muted thudding of hooves in the dirt. Jacob tried not to let his anxiety show. The white man was quiet, lost in thought, but Jacob knew how quickly that could change.

"There is a fresh shipment of slaves coming in, from French Africa. I could do with your help Jacob. I want you to look at them with me, talk with them. I want you to help me decide which will be strong, which will work well."

The demand hit Jacob almost physically in his belly. Could the white man not see the injustice? Jacob shook his head imperceptibly at the inhumanity.

"Yes master."

Again the white man was lost in thought.
They rode further in silence, before he spoke
again.

"Jacob, I could do with some more help up at
the house. I need someone I can depend on.
I've decided to move you up to the house with
me and my family. You can do jobs, drive the
trap, do what I need you to do. No more work
in the fields for you now. How do you like
that, eh?

"Yes master."

***

Under the grey, cloud-laden sky, the dirty
white frontage of the Keppel's Head looked
particularly drab and uninviting. Rain
dropped in swollen globules from the tattered
eaves. Once again Kitty knocked on the door
of the hotel, with more confidence than the
last time. The door opened a crack, and then
wider, the moustachioed innkeeper greeting
them with almost obsequious civility.
"Why, if it isn't my young friends again?
And with another young urchin to join you.
How pleased Mr Peabody will be! Step this
way young lady and gentlemen. Step this
way please."

Kitty turned her face away to avoid the stench of his breath. She noticed that Philip showed no compunction in seating himself on one of the plushly upholstered chairs, and, deciding she would not be outdone, she joined him. Charlie, looking slightly less sure of himself, stood, shifting uneasily from foot to foot.

"Come, come, my young gentlefolk. You look as if you might be hungry. I will see if we have anything in the kitchen for you. What do you say? Hmm? A little morsel to eat?"

They stared distrustfully back at him, but, unabashed, the innkeeper disappeared, returning moments later with a somewhat small basket of pastries. As if he had produced some culinary masterpiece the innkeeper exclaimed,

"Feast, my children, feast on that. Don't ever say I don't feed you well in this here establishment! Now, if you would like to wait here, I will alert the gentleman that you have arrived."

They did not have long to wait before they heard the sound of footsteps on the stairs above - first the ungainly shuffle of the innkeeper, followed by a lighter sharper tread, as if each foot was positioned, with careful precision, before the other lifted. The door opened and Mr Peabody unfolded himself into the room, his gangly frame stooping beneath the building's low ceiling.

"Ah, my two young adventurers. We meet once again. And how are you faring in your quest?"

He broke off, staring at Philip.

"Young Master Pemberton, how glad I am to see you alive and unharmed! What pleasure it gives me to see you so well, what pleasure indeed!"

Philip, Kitty could see, was somewhat taken aback by the man's advances. He spoke uncertainly, as if unsure of his own recollections.

"Who are you sir? Do I know you? And if so, please tell me how?"

Mr Peabody's expression changed from its habitual enthusiasm to a solemn earnestness.

"I am – was – a good friend of your mother's. We knew each other a long time ago. I have not seen her for some years, but we have always kept in contact via letters. I last saw you when you were a tiny baby, and here you are all grown up. I was so sorry to hear what happened to your mother, so sorry."

Philip still looked distrustful, and his face darkened at the mention of his mother.

"And who are you? How do I know I can trust you?"

Mr Peabody's sombre expression lightened slightly.

"Ah, a sensible question from a bright lad. Philip, your mother knew she was in danger. I said that we corresponded by letter. She sent me, just a few months ago, a letter that I was to show to you, by way of introduction, if anything were to befall her."

He reached into his inner jacket pocket and pulled out a letter, folded over on itself, which he proceeded to smooth out and passed to Philip.

My dearest Philip,

If you are reading this letter then I fear that the worst has happened, and I am no longer with you. It also means that you are in danger. You can trust the man who bears this letter. His name is Mr Samuel Peabody, and he is an old friend. He will look after you.

I love you so much my darling. I am sorry to leave you this way. I have watched you grow, every day, every month, every year, and I am so, so proud of you. Whatever happens, and whatever befalls you, always remind yourself how much I love you. Your loving mother,

Eliza Pemberton

Philip finished the letter and carefully folded it, keeping it clutched tightly in his hand. Unshed tears glistened in his eyes as he looked up at them.

"She knew she was in danger. She knew and she never told me about it."

Philip stifled a sob in the back of his throat.

"What has happened to you Philip? Tell me about it."

Mr Peabody's voice was gentle.

"I don't know that much. My father disappeared five days ago. He went off one evening to a meeting and never came back. My mother was beside herself with worry. But there was more than that. It was as if she'd been expecting something like this to happen. She seemed terrified, but not surprised. The next morning she announced that we would have to come to Portsmouth. We took a coach that day and arrived early in the evening. There was someone here that she had to see. I don't know who."

He broke off and looked at Mr Peabody hopefully.

"Was that you, Mr Peabody?"

Mr Peabody nodded and Philip continued.

"After we alighted, Mother said there was a bit of a walk. We'd had a long, uncomfortable coach journey, and she thought it would do us both good."

Philip broke off for a moment and breathed deeply.

"It was getting dark and we had to walk across a long common. Mother led me down a side-street and that's where they came for us. There were two men. I think they must have followed us. They jumped out at us in the dark and grabbed my mother. She screamed at me to run, so I did. One of them tried to grab me, the shorter one. But I wriggled free and got away."

"Would you recognise them? The men that attacked you?"

Philip shook his head.

"I don't think so. It was very dark. The tall one I hardly saw. I don't think I'd know him again. The one that grabbed me had a scar. A horrible scar across his face. That I might recognise."

Mr Peabody nodded again.

"Good, good. We may catch them yet. Well my young friend you have had a remarkable escape. I will take care of you for the moment, while we see if we can contact your father. You have been through a lot of terrible things, but now you are safe. Come upstairs and we will have you bathed and cleaned up in no time."

Mr Peabody stood, and Philip looked uncertainly at Kitty and Charlie.

"You don't have to worry anymore," said Kitty, more brightly than she felt. "You go with Mr Peabody. He'll look after you."

Mr Peabody held out a shilling each to Kitty and Charlie.

"And you two, my thanks to both of you. A shilling each hardly covers the great service that you have done me, but please, take it anyway as a token of my gratitude. I – we – are greatly indebted to you."

Kitty and Charlie took the shillings, but without eagerness. Somehow Kitty felt a reluctance to leave, even though the mystery was solved and Philip was safe. There didn't seem anything else to do however, so she and Charlie took their leave and were ushered out by the unpleasant, and now unsmiling, innkeeper.

"Right you two, scram! Mr Peabody may have a soft spot for you but don't think you can be coming back again and bothering all my guests. If you do I'll have you both locked up quicker than you can say 'street urchin'."

Kitty and Charlie raced down the steps to the street. Kitty looked back at the hotel. The last thing she saw was Philip, waving disconsolately to them from an upstairs window.

Chapter 7

"We can't stop now Kitty. We still don't know what's going on."

Kitty had to admit she felt a sense of disappointment, of unfinished business, that had only grown since they left Philip with Mr Peabody.

They trudged through the rain in the direction of Kitty's home. Kitty knew that Charlie would only put off his own return. Things were never good where he lived, and she knew enough to read the signs. The bruise from the previous day had deepened to an angry purple and yellow. Most of the time he showed no sign of noticing it, but occasionally, caught at an unwary moment, he would wince as he turned his neck, stretching the mottled skin.

"Does it hurt much?" Kitty asked solicitously as his mouth twisted.

He shook his head, wincing again involuntarily.

"No. Not too bad. Not as bad as what I'll do to him if he doesn't leave her alone in future."

Somehow the aggressive words didn't quite ring true coming from Charlie. He seemed to sense her scepticism and shrugged.

"Ok, not as bad as what I'd like to do to him if I catch him."

"Who is he? Where has he gone?"

Again Charlie shrugged.

"Who is he? Just the latest in the line. Where's he gone? As far away as possible, I hope. But there'll be more…" he added sadly.

"When's your da back?"

Kitty suspected that the casual shoulder shrug belied Charlie's real feelings.

"Don't know. Not for a while maybe. Anyway, it's no better when he is back. He's just as bad. In fact, he's worse than some of them."

Charlie looked so desolate that Kitty couldn't help but put an arm around his shoulders. He leaned into her and closed his eyes for a moment. Then suddenly he straightened and his face hardened to the world once again.

"Come on, let's get you home."

"What will you do?"

"I don't know yet. I'm not going home, that's for sure. I might go back to the Flathouse Rookery. We still need to know more about Mr Chamberlain. Anyway, I'll think of something and let you know."

"Why don't you come to ours first and have something to eat. My mother would be glad enough to see you. Then we can make a plan."

Charlie looked gratefully at her and nodded. "Thanks."

Kitty thought she saw the hardness slip from his face for a moment but he turned slightly away so she couldn't see. They walked on in silence.

As they approached Kitty's street, Charlie put out an arm and stopped her. In the small cobbled yard between the houses they saw a pair of familiar figures. The tall, thin figure stood back, as if enjoying the spectacle, while the shorter man with the scar remonstrated earnestly with Kitty's father. Kitty's father was standing his ground, hands on hips, his face suffused with fury. Kitty and Charlie shrank back, unseen, into the shadows.

"What do we do now?" hissed Charlie.

Kitty thought for a moment.

"The rookery."

***

They ran through the rain, heedless of the filthy water splashing against their legs. They kept running till they reached the Unicorn Gate, then slowed to a more cautious walk. Hesitantly they entered the rookery, Kitty trying to remember their way through the labyrinth of boardwalks and paths. They were both nervous, looking continually over their shoulders, as if expecting to be challenged at any moment. This was not their territory. Last time they had been allowed in by Polly. This time they were intruders.

Kitty struggled a few times to remember the directions but she was surprised by Charlie's recall. It took them longer than before, but eventually they found the ramshackle wooden building where they'd met Philip.

Approaching cautiously, they once again heard a low whistle. Moments later their way was barred by a group of boys and girls, about five in total. Kitty recognised one of them as Flynn, the boy they met on their last visit.

"What do you want?"

"We need to see Polly. Polly Perkins."

"Never heard of 'er. Who are you?"

"I'm Kitty Hawkins. And this is Charlie Miller. We were here yesterday. We met you Flynn, don't you remember?"

The boy's eyes narrowed.

"Never seen you before. Don't know what you're talkin' about."

Kitty didn't know what to do. She had been unsure about coming to the rookery, but hadn't expected this reception.

"Please, please, help us. We were here yesterday. And we took Philip to Mr Peabody. But now we're in trouble and the police are chasing us. Please help us."

Another whistle sounded from behind them. They turned and Kitty's heart leapt as she saw Polly Perkins.

"It's all right folks. Leave 'em alone. They won't do us no harm. You two! In 'ere!"

She gestured for them to follow her with an inclination of her head, and disappeared into the building. Kitty and Charlie pushed past the dirty curtain and into the dingy gloom. Polly sat on a makeshift wooden stool. She stared hard at them as they entered.

"What's up with you two then? Didn't expect to see you so quickly?"

She didn't seem suspicious, but inquisitive, and Kitty explained all that had happened. Polly listened attentively throughout, occasionally firing a question at one or the other of them, before lapsing back to silence. Eventually Kitty ran out of words. Polly waited till she dried up before speaking.

"You can stay here if you like. We can't protect you but we can hide you. But what about your parents? Will they be worried?"

Kitty was surprised at the insight from the tough street urchin. Charlie laughed drily.

"Not mine. My da could be anywhere and my ma could be with anyone. The only thing she'd miss would be the money I bring in." Polly looked at him with sympathetic solidarity. Kitty shook her head worriedly. "My mother will be beside herself, I know. I must get a message to her."

Polly smiled.

"I'm sure we can manage that. But what are we going to do about the police?"

In the silence that followed it was Charlie that spoke first.

"Chamberlain. We've got to find this mysterious Mr Chamberlain. As long as he's out there, those police will be chasing us. He's the key to all of this."

***

Darkness had settled on Portsea as they crept through the narrow streets. There were few street lights, but the lamps in the houses glimmered and shone on the wet cobbles, giving enough light to see by. Polly went ahead. She was used to not being seen, and the police wouldn't recognise her (although, as she had explained, over the years she had become well-acquainted with them). Kitty and Charlie couldn't help admiring the way she moved through the streets, effortlessly flitting from shadow to shadow. Kitty had thought herself good at staying unnoticed, but she quickly realised that Polly was a cut above her in stealth.

They reached the small courtyard into which Kitty's house opened. In the dark, the grey brick terraces loomed above them, plunging them into deepening gloom. It had been agreed that Polly would knock on the door. That way she could invent an innocent enquiry, should their pursuers be present. Polly broke out of her shadow and marched up to the door that Kitty indicated. She rapped sharply and waited. A few moments later the door opened a crack and Kitty's heart leapt as she saw her father's face illuminated in the space.

"Hello Mr Hawkins. I'm Polly. A friend of Kitty's."

Immediately there was a scuffle inside and Kitty's mother appeared at the doorway, flinging it open wide.

"Have you news of Kitty? Do you know where she is? Oh, please tell me!"

Kitty's father looked appraisingly at Polly. "You know that the police are looking for Kitty?"

"Yes. Are they here."

"No. They left hours ago. They didn't seem to know where to start looking."

At this Kitty could contain herself no longer. She burst from the shadows and ran to her parents. Charlie followed. After a momentary look of surprise, Kitty's mother hugged her hard, almost suffocating her.

"Kitty. You're safe! Thank the Lord!"

"Come inside now, all of you. It's not safe out here."

Kitty's father hustled them all through the door, into the dim warmth of the lamp-lit house. Polly and Charlie sat on Kitty's bedroll. Kitty's mother seemed reluctant to let go of her. She held her closely. It was obvious that she had been crying.

"So, Kitty. Tell us what is happening. One night you come home late, covered in mud. The next minute the police are here looking for you. What is going on?"

Kitty looked at Polly. She looked at Charlie. They both stared silently at the floor. She took a deep breath. Then she began to talk. At first the words came falteringly, but gradually, gathering momentum, they flooded out. She told them about Philip, Mr Peabody, Philip's mother, and how they had found her body, lying in the stinking mud. She told them everything.

Eventually the words dried up. She looked nervously up at her parents. Her mother looked shocked. Her father's expression was hard to read.

"Well it's a strange story, and no mistake. What do you plan to do?"

"We're staying up with Polly, at Flathouse Rookery. She's hiding us."

At the mention of the rookery her mother gasped.

"Don't fear mother. We have friends there. We're safer there than anywhere at the moment. It's the one place the police won't find us."

Her father nodded.

"Aye, that's probably true. You're safer there than you are here with us. The police'll be back here before you know it, snooping around. They're saying you were seen with the lady's corpse. They've not accused you of any crime yet Kitty, but you mustn't let them catch you. They'll string you up without a second thought."

Again her mother gasped.

"But... but... can't we explain? Can't we tell them that Kitty's innocent? Can't we at least keep her here, safe where we can see her?"

It hadn't occurred to Kitty's mother that she might not be innocent, Kitty noticed gratefully.

"No Alice, we can't keep her safe here. Do you think that's the last we've seen of our two friends from the police? They'll be back, and they'll pull this place apart looking for her. Kitty's right. She's got to stay away. As for telling them Kitty is innocent, who will they believe? I don't know who is behind this, but you can bet they've got the police and the courts in their pocket. Do you think they'll listen to us?"

Kitty's mother acquiesced.

"No, I suppose you're right. But I'm so scared. Oh Kitty, do be so careful. I can't bear the thought of anything happening to you. Not after… not after Joshua."

Kitty's mother broke off, turning away and holding one hand up to her face. When she looked back her eyes were overly bright and glistening gently in the lamplight. This time she looked at Polly and Charlie.

"Please look after her. Promise me you'll watch over her. She's all I've got."

***

Kitty's father fetched the cups off the fire. The coffee was bitter, but the warmth flooding through them was delicious. Kitty's mother was busy preparing packages of food for them to take with them. Polly looked as if she'd never seen such luxury (which, incidentally, she hadn't), and was fighting her own instincts to help a few of the smaller items in the house escape in her pockets.

"Now, tell me. What are you going to do about this secret order and Mr Chamberlain?" Kitty's father crossed his arms and leaned back, trying not to let the excitement or the worry show. Kitty had shown him the twisted scarlet ribbon that she still carried, but he had been as baffled as Mr Pounds. Kitty couldn't think what to do. She had been so focused on seeing her parents that she hadn't thought much beyond this. She looked at Charlie and smiled. He was doing a fair imitation of her father's gruff pragmatism.

"We can spread the word - see if anyone's heard about it. We might be better off looking for Mr Chamberlain though. We're more likely to pick up something about him." Kitty nodded and started to speak but Polly butted in across her.

"What about your Mr Peabody? He seems to know a lot that he's not telling us. Why don't we start by asking him?"

Kitty nodded again.

"It's a good idea. As long as we can reach him without being caught."

Polly smiled.

"Course we can! You can leave that to me. I'll get us past anyone."

Kitty's father looked up and smiled.

"Yes Polly, I believe you could. Like Alice says, please look after them. They're brave enough but I worry we all may be a little out of our depth. Now, Kitty I must go and comfort your mother for a while. Don't leave without saying goodbye."

He turned towards the stairwell leading to the upstairs bedroom. Polly looked at Kitty.

"Who's Joshua?"

"What?" Kitty was caught off-guard.

"You heard me. Your mother mentioned Joshua. Who is he?"

Kitty looked for a moment as if she was going to argue, then shrugged.

"He was my brother. He died, three years ago. He was only four years old. My mother's never been the same since."

"I'm sorry."

You could read the interest competing with the sympathy on Polly's face.

"What happened."

Kitty made a face.

"I don't really know. He just got sick. It all happened very quickly. He didn't last long." She didn't often talk about it, particularly around her parents, and the memory of her brother was surprisingly painful. Polly's face softened. They're lucky they've got you, you know. And you're lucky you've got them. They're good people, your parents."

Charlie broke his silence, his voice unusually thick and heavy.

"I think I'd like to see my mother after all. Polly, can you get us there safely?"

***

It all happened very quickly. One day he was a happy, healthy little boy. A few days later he was dead. It wasn't unusual. Most of the people they knew had lost a child at some stage. The neighbours were wary of them for a few weeks, but once it was clear that none of them were sickening they forgot their caution. In some ways, Kitty thought, life should have returned to normal then. But it couldn't. Of course it couldn't.

It took her months to really believe he was gone. It wasn't that she'd paid him a great deal of attention when he was alive. But once he was gone she really noticed the hole in her life. At first she would wake each morning, initially forgetting, or thinking she had dreamt his death. Then each morning as memory settled in she relived the loss afresh. Eventually his absence became part of the background of her life. She attended her lessons, sold her candles and talked to Charlie. Not to her mother. Joshua's absence wasn't real to her mother. Often Kitty overheard her mother talking to Joshua. Once she tried to join in, but her mother looked embarrassed and wouldn't let her. It was a pity. She would have liked to join in. Sometimes she tried talking to him when she was on her own. He never answered, but she hoped he could hear her.

Joshua was gone. But he was still there. Still in the house. Her mother kept him alive, but the effort took her away from them all. She wasn't just distant from Kitty she was distant from the world, as if she was seeing another world, far away, hearing other voices. Then at other times she would return and cling desperately to her daughter, hugging her with a fierce, almost frantic intensity. Meanwhile her father just carried on, much the same but slightly slower, slightly sadder. Kitty still had his love, but she missed his laughter.

***

It didn't take them long to reach Charlie's place. Geographically the distance wasn't great although, Kitty reflected, in other ways the gulf was huge. As they walked, the streets grew busier, despite the late hour, and the sounds of raucous revelry echoed in their ears. From the sides of the street strangers eyed them as they passed.

"You're a pretty thing dear. Step over here and have a talk with old Sally." Kitty looked towards the voice calling her. The woman stood behind a small brazier, swinging a half-full bottle in her hands. Her face was cracked and peeling and she was missing most of her front teeth, but somehow the voice didn't sound as old as its owner. Polly steered her on.

"This one's not for you Sally. Leave us alone."

"You never were much fun Polly, God bless yer!" cackled the old lady.

Near to Charlie's house the streets were dirtier. A couple of stray dogs fought over a dead animal. From the putrid smell that emanated as they passed, Kitty guessed it had been dead for a while. As they trudged through the thick layer of accumulated muck

Kitty felt the occasional movement of a rat across the top of her feet and shuddered. Charlie didn't seem to notice, but his face hardened as they reached the row of buildings where his mother lived.

Charlie pushed open the door to his mother's room. The stench of filth was overpowering. Sweat and excrement assaulted the nostrils immediately. His mother lay on the floor, snoring loudly. There was a bed in the corner, but she clearly hadn't made it that far. The sheets were thrown back messily, and looked as though they had not been washed in years. Even Polly looked slightly shocked. For Charlie it was all too familiar.

He walked over to where his mother lay, picking his way carefully through the detritus that lined the floor. He shook her gently.

"Mother! Mother! It's me. Charlie."

She didn't wake so he shook her again, this time a little more firmly.

"Mother! Wake up. It's me."

This time his mother opened her eyes and stared at him blearily.

"Charlie? Charlie?"

She began to cry. Charlie cradled her head for a few minutes on his knees. Eventually she pulled herself up into a sitting position.

"You always were a good boy, Charlie. Get your old ma a drink will you?"

Charlie looked around at the empty gin bottle rolling on the floor. She'd had plenty of that already, he decided. He found a cup and filled it from the standpipe outside in the courtyard. She swilled it distastefully in her mouth but didn't spit it out. Instead she looked up at him hopefully.

"Got anything stronger, to pick me spirits up?"

Charlie ignored the comment.

"Mother, where's… where's…" he sought for the name of the last sailor who had stayed here, "Frank?"

She looked about her self-pityingly.

"He's gone. They've all gone. All but you Charlie. You're the only one that cares."

He helped her into a chair and slowly, gently, put the cup to her lips. Sip by tiny sip he coaxed her to finish the cup, and when it was drained he quickly returned with a refill. She had a couple of bluish bruises to her own face and what looked like the marks of fingers imprinted on her bare arms.

"Did he do this to you? Frank, I mean."

She nodded wordlessly.

"Why do you let them, mother? They shouldn't do this to you."

She wouldn't meet his eye as she replied.

"He wasn't always like that. He looked after me at first you know. Gave me money. Bought me things. Bought us things. We shouldn't be too ungrateful. But now he's gone…"

She began to weep, her shoulders shaking silently. Charlie couldn't be sure if she'd been talking about Frank or his father. It was much the same, he reflected. The same promises. The same problems. The same violence.

"Mother, I can't stay. It's too dangerous. The police are looking for me."

For the first time his mother seemed to bring the world into proper focus. She looked at him anxiously.

"Charlie, my Charlie. What have you done? Why are they looking for you?"

"Don't worry mum. I've done nothing wrong." Charlie sounded more confident than he felt.

"It's all a mistake. You'll see. But just for the moment you've got to be strong. I'll be back with you soon."

His mother started weeping again and clutched at his neck.

"Charlie, Charlie, don't go. I can't do without you."

Charlie gently detached himself, and pressed Mr Peabody's shilling into her palm.

"Here's some money to be going on with mother. It's all I've got. But I'll be back with more as soon as I can."

She started to thank him, sniffing through her tears, but already her eyes darted to the empty gin bottle. Charlie sighed. He knew where his money would go, and it wouldn't be on food. But what else could he do? He looked up at Polly and Kitty.

"Let's go."

***

Once more they knocked at the door of the Keppel's Head. This time the faded and peeling paintwork was illuminated by the dull glow of lanterns, spitting in the cascading rain. Once more the yellow-toothed, beer-breathed innkeeper grudgingly opened the door, and stared at them, this time more venomously than usual.

"You lot again! Didn't I tell you what would happen if you came round here, botherin' my clients? I'll set the police on you, that's what I'll do!"

"Please, sir, please. We need to see Mr
Peabody. We need his advice, desperately."
"Mr Peabody ain't here. He's gone. Now I
suggest you go too before I set my dog on
you."
Kitty stopped in her tracks. Mr Peabody had
gone? Where had he gone? And why? And
what had happened to Philip? She needed to
know.
"Please sir, please, can you tell us where he's
gone. Was Philip with him? The young lad
we brought here."
The man's eyes narrowed.
"I don't know where he's gone, or whether
he's taken that young varmint with him. But
he's gone. Now I told you to scram. Go!"
This time, sensing there may not be many
more chances, they took his advice and raced
away.

***

Samuel Peabody leaned out of the coach
window and looked up at the driver.
"Can't you go any faster?" he called out,
irritably. The coach's wheels bumped on the
uneven cobbles, jarring his spine. As he
spoke, he recognised the futility of his

137

question. The coach was suffering enough at the speed they were going.

"No sir, that I can't, not unless you wants to be walking the rest of the way!" called the coach-driver cheerfully.

Mr Peabody drew himself back into the carriage and looked at the boy, sleeping on the plush blue upholstery. The boy had been through a lot, an awful lot. But he knew there was more to come. Might as well let him sleep for the time being. He thought of Kitty Hawkins. She would look for him. He was sure of that. Would she find him? He couldn't be sure. She was bright and resourceful. He wouldn't be surprised if he saw her again.

The boy opposite him stirred and moved an arm in his sleep. Mr Peabody remained still, unwilling to disturb the boy's rest. He thought about the boy's mother. It was a pity, such a pity. She had been a beautiful and intelligent woman. He had admired her greatly.

He looked out of the window, watching the rain-washed Portsmouth streets slip by. It would not be long now before it was all over. He noticed the tiny droplets running down the pane of the coach-window, forking and diverting with every slight imperfection in the glass. For a moment he focussed on the detail, the way the raindrops caught the light and the tangled patterns they traced. Gradually the detail blurred and his gaze returned to the world beyond.

**

1831

Jamaica

The burning was intense. The dry timber frames of the buildings blazed fiercely in the Caribbean heat. Despite the flames Jacob shivered in fear. Memories crowded in on him, unwanted and unbidden: the burning buildings; the stench of smoke; the overwhelming chaos. He fought the urge to run. Sweat glistened on his forehead, mingling with the white ash. The shouting had died out, receding into the distance as fast as it had arrived. Jacob looked at the devastation left in its wake. The buildings were consumed, burning shells in the midst of the cane fields. The cart that he had driven, only yesterday, stood on its side, wheel rims hanging loosely from their splintered spokes, the barrels smashed in the yard where they had fallen, rolling forlornly in the breeze. Jacob was conscious of a vague ache from his innards. He could not locate the source of his disquiet, but neither could he escape the feeling that he had fallen short that day. He looked around him at the devastation, with a growing sense that something momentous had just happened. His brothers and sisters had risen up. But what had he done? He had not fought them, but neither had he joined them. He had survived, but at what cost?

Beneath the cart his eye caught a flicker of movement. He hastened to investigate. As he crouched to look into the dark space, a small, frightened pair of eyes stared back at him.

"Jacob?"

The word was no more than a whisper, yet sounded unbearably loud in the deafening silence of the yard, accompanied only by the gentle crackle of flames. He silenced her with a finger to his lips, looking quickly around for signs of danger. Seeing nothing he reached in with his arms and pulled the terrified child out. She clung to him, trusting but fearful.

"Don't you worry Miss Elizabeth. Now, don't you worry, we'll find your folks see, and then things'll all be just fine."

She looked up at him, placed her tiny white hand in his. He gripped it reassuringly. He led her gently, almost tenderly down the slope, towards the one remaining building. The old stone barn, nearest to the cane fields, had somehow escaped the chaos and conflagration.

"Look Miss Elizabeth. I'll get you settled in the barn, make you real comfortable. Then I'll find your ma and pa, I promise."

"What if the bad men come back."

Jacob thought about the men, the bad men. No, they were not bad but desperate - driven to violence by years in chains. He thought about their struggle, and their sacrifice, and wondered what would happen now. A vague sense of foreboding washed over him. Whatever came of this, for good or ill, he feared that far more suffering lay ahead.

"Don't worry Miss Elizabeth. They won't come back."

The little girl smiled trustingly up at him and allowed herself to be led down the track. As they walked she sang to herself, a gentle childish tune. Jacob could barely make out the words, but the melody haunted him, sounding so pure amidst the wreckage surrounding them, rising quietly but clearly *above the hiss and crackle of the dying flames.*

The track led through the yard and down a short slope towards the barn. To the left the stable block smouldered, the horses having long since bolted in terror. He had at least managed to untie the horses. It was small consolation, but it was some comfort to his battered conscience.

He sensed the white man's movement before he saw him. He stood from the stable embers, rifle raised.

"Jacob!"

Jacob stopped, unable to break the habit of servitude, and turned to face the white man.

"Jacob! What are you doing?"

"Taking Miss Elizabeth to the barn master. Taking Miss Elizabeth somewhere safe."

"Step away from Elizabeth, Jacob! Let go of the child or I'll shoot you where you stand."

Jacob let go of the girl's hand. Her trusting face crumpled as she tried vainly to make sense of the situation.

"No father! Please father, Jacob was helping me. Jacob was looking after me. Please, please don't hurt him."

Her voice was a wail, rising to a crescendo of fear as the terror of the day welled up within her. The white man continued to stare down his rifle at Jacob. Jacob raised his face to the white man's and met his gaze.

"What do you think? That I would hurt a child? Shoot me if you will, but do not think that of me."

They stood facing each other, held in speechless tension, even the child transfixed in silence. Eventually the white man lowered his rifle.

"All right Jacob, take Miss Elizabeth to the barn. Make her comfortable and then come back and help me. Let's start clearing up this mess."

It was not an apology, but it was the closest he would get.

Chapter 8

They sat in the Flathouse Rookery listening to the rain beat on the roof. It had been raining for two days now and the town was awash, the city sewers having long since surrendered to the onslaught. The flooding flushed out the bodies of vermin and other animals, and the corpses lay rotting in the watery roadside. Portsmouth stank.

Other than the stench, Kitty was adjusting to her new accommodation. Most of the other Flathouse children had accepted them without question. Polly accepted them, so they were accepted. Well, almost accepted. Kitty looked across to where Flynn lay with his back to them. He had avoided them since their arrival. On the odd occasions that he was forced to address them, it would inevitably be with a malicious humour. As if he could feel Kitty's eyes on his back the boy rolled over to look at her.

"Any ideas, clever girl?"

Kitty couldn't help bristling slightly at Flynn's teasing. So far their scouts had brought no news of the Scarlet Order or of Mr Chamberlain or of Mr Peabody. They seemed to have reached a complete standstill.

"If you're going to help, Flynn, then come and help. If not, keep your nose out of it."
Flynn grunted, and rolled back away from them.

"Huh! Suit yourself. Why should I care about your posh little friend anyway?"
Kitty ignored him and turned to the others.
"I don't understand why Mr Peabody went away. And what's happened to Philip? I hope he's alright."
Polly looked across at Kitty.
"He's probably gone back to London with young Philip in tow. I'm sure they're fine. Anyway, Flynn's got a point. Why are you so worried about the youngster? You don't really know him after all."
"I know Polly, but I still feel responsible for him. After all, we took him to Mr Peabody in the first place. And we still don't know what happened to his parents, or why."
They sat quietly for a few moments, huddled in their own thoughts. Polly poked the small fire burning in the brazier, turning the glowing embers over and watching the tiny sparks spit and fizzle out in the air. As she stared at the dancing pinpricks of light, Kitty felt the glimmerings of an idea take shape in her mind.

"We can't find Peabody or Philip. We don't know who Chamberlain is. But there are two people we can find, so let's start with them." Everyone stared at her.

"The two policemen I mean. They can't be hard to find. After all, we know they're looking for us. I think it's time we stopped hiding and started hunting."

***

Mr Chamberlain looked at the assembled company before him. The atmosphere was formal but polite. He was under no illusions that each of these people would happily see him dead, if it were advantageous to them. But at the moment they needed him alive. He smiled inwardly at the ostentatious splendour of their surroundings. The medieval torches, in brackets against the thick stone walls, were no doubt intended to add a certain gravitas to the occasion. Their dark robes were plain, adorned only by a single twist of scarlet ribbon, pinned to the left breast. The decorative masks they wore to disguise their faces may have hinted at a certain mystique. But Mr Chamberlain was not one to be concerned with such fripperies.

"The boy has been moved. He will be hard for anyone to get at now."

The assembled company nodded.

"And what of your…" the masked conspirator paused, "… colleagues?"

"One will not be a threat to us. The others are being taken care of."

Mr Chamberlain's face remained impassive beneath his mask. The mask annoyed him intensely. He did not need to conceal his face to disappear.

"This is a delicate situation Mr Chamberlain. We would be most… displeased if anything… untoward should happen."

Joseph Chamberlain scowled. What did they think would happen? Did they expect him to fear their threats? For a moment he visualised the chess-board, covered in their masked figures. His voice returned to its most urbane and ingratiating.

"Of course gentlemen, as, I can assure you would I. But you may rest assured that every eventuality has been anticipated and every provision made, for all our safety."

He allowed the last word to ring, slightly over-accentuated, not quite a threat, but certainly the hint of one. He watched in amusement as his companions shifted uneasily in their seats. He could smell their anxiety. Let them worry!

"Our concern is only for the good of the order Mr Chamberlain. This must always be our key priority."

Joseph Chamberlain looked at the speaker. His ceremonial robes could not hide his large girth, nor the throaty rasp of his voice, and Joseph did not need to strip the mask away to guess at his identity. He smiled sardonically.

"I quite understand, Grand Master Walpole. The good of the order must always come first. Now if you gentlemen will excuse me I have work to do."

He turned on his heel and swept from the hall, anticipating with amusement the chaos he would leave in his wake.

"Who does he think he is? Daring to address the Grand Master by name! Does he have no respect for the traditions and secrecy of our order?"

"He has little respect for anyone if you ask me."

It was true. He didn't have much respect for the order, and even less for those in it. But for now it was a necessary encumbrance. The fools had far too much faith in their own importance. They thought they could get away with anything and the order would protect them. They were happy for him to do their dirty work, as long as it never came back to them. But soon they would find their misdeeds returning, and with interest.

**

Tobias Samuelson lay in the roadside and pondered his life as it ran away from him. It had happened very quickly. He had felt only a gentle, but sharp sensation across his throat and his legs had lost all power as his companion lowered him to the floor. He had tried to speak, to call out, but no sound came, save for the bubbling from his neck.

He had never been an ambitious man. The call to the constabulary had been one of self-indulgent opportunism rather than conviction, he was the first to admit. The job had been comfortable and, for a man of his limited talents, rather well-paid. Added to that was a certain status, which he had not been afraid to avail himself of when it had suited him.

As a man of greater pragmatism than principle, he had not been averse to the occasional acceptance of financial recompense for such services as 'looking the other way' and 'not seeing what was right in front of his nose'. However this last job had unsettled him from the start. He would not have done it at all had it not been for the earnest encouragement of his colleague and friend, Mr Bartholomew.

Of course once he had been drawn in he had quickly realised that there was no way out. He was chilled by the urbane and unspoken threat of Mr Chamberlain. They had killed a woman. Even Tobias's ever-adaptable code of morality could not quite encompass that. Tobias considered all these things in the time it took for his eyes to dull. But as the blood escaped from his cleanly cut throat, they seemed to matter less and less. And, at the last, all he could see was the image of his friend, Mr Bartholomew, and the gentle caress of his voice as the light faded.

***

Jerome Bartholomew was an un-empathetic man by nature. He felt no great sense of guilt at the despatch of his erstwhile colleague and friend, Mr Samuelson. Nonetheless, he realised that the hastening of Tobias's untimely demise had not been the most companionly of actions. As he walked from the still-warm body of his friend he dropped the knife to the floor. He had no further use for it, and being caught with the murder weapon was a beginner's mistake. He looked quickly around him for any prying eyes and then walked away without looking back.

The last killing, he knew, had been clumsy. That, he blamed on Tobias. But nonetheless, they had been spotted. This was something that must not happen again. He would see to it that nothing went wrong now.

Mr Bartholomew hurried through the night without looking over his shoulder. He would have to wait for a while. He knew he could disappear if he needed to, but to do so now would only arouse suspicion. No, he would stay and play his part, waiting and watching for the right moment. Besides, he still had those children to deal with.

***

When Polly put the word out onto the street, the word spread quickly. By the afternoon every mud-lark, hawker[2] and street-sweeper in the city knew that Polly was looking for the two policemen. Kitty and Charlie were amazed at her network of spies.

---

[2] Hawker: Someone who travels about selling goods.

"I always thought you knew everyone Charlie!" exclaimed Kitty. Charlie smiled. "So did I, but Polly's got the whole town in her hand. She's amazing."

Kitty caught the tone of admiration in his voice and looked up sharply, a sarcastic retort hovering on her lips. She stopped herself. She had to admit it. Polly *was* incredible. But for some reason she didn't want Charlie thinking Polly was *too* incredible.

The steady stream of boys and girls continued through the day, bringing their whispered reports to Polly. But each report was the same. The men were nowhere to be found.

"How hard can it be? A few days ago we couldn't shake them off." grumbled Charlie. Flynn heard him and shot over a malevolent look.

"Stop complaining mud-boy. Why do you want to meet the police so much anyway?" Charlie swore at him, but the younger boy had already gone, ducking out of a window and disappearing into the rookery. He might enjoy making Charlie and Kitty's lives uncomfortable, but he would do what Polly said. And he was good. Really good. According to Polly, Flynn had the sharpest eyes on the street. He could spot an unguarded wallet with his eyes closed. And he could almost smell the police, long before they noticed him. It was a rare talent and one that had saved him from the magistrates on many an occasion.

It was early evening before Flynn returned. Looking up from where she and Charlie had been discussing Philip's whereabouts, Kitty bit back her comments. Flynn's face was grim. Not malevolent this time. Just grim.

"Have you found something?" Kitty asked uncertainly.

Flynn nodded. He walked over to Polly and Kitty and Charlie followed.

"I've found your copper."

"Which one?" asked Kitty.

Flynn glared at her and addressed his answer to Polly.

"The fat one with the scar. Not that he'll be much use to you."

"Go on…" said Polly.

"He's dead. I found him round the back of Spice Island. He can't have been there long. The maggots hadn't got him yet. Or the pickpockets!"

Flynn held up a cheap leather purse which he emptied on the table. A couple of coins rolled out. He laughed scornfully at Kitty's disapproving look.

"Too good to rob a dead man are you girl? Well listen to me, when you've been as hungry as I have you'll rob anyone, dead or alive. So don't pretend to be all high and mighty on me now."

"Was it an accident?" Polly looked like she knew the answer to her own question. Flynn shook his head.

"Someone slit his throat. Ear to ear. Didn't look much like an accident to me."

***

Kitty scratched her knuckles against the wall, frustratedly. They had been cooped up in the rookery all day, waiting while other people scoured the city for their quarry. She wanted to get out there and do something. But Polly was right. If people were looking for them, they were better staying safe, here in Flathouse. She knew Polly was right, but it didn't stop her begrudging it.

Charlie seemed to be more relaxed. Content even. That annoyed Kitty even more. Every time one of Polly's informants arrived he hung around her (slightly unnecessarily Kitty thought) asking questions.

She couldn't help thinking about the dead policeman. She remembered him when he had chased her and Charlie. He hadn't struck her as a particularly dangerous man. Unpleasant perhaps, but not dangerous. But he had been, it seemed. Had he really killed Philip's mother? Or had he too been mixed up in something that became more dangerous than he was prepared for?

When she had talked to Charlie about it Flynn had overheard her. As usual he treated her with cold disdain.

"Hah! Feeling sorry for the copper are you? Should have known it. Well you cry for your copper all you like but don't come snivelling to me when they put a noose round your neck and watch you swing."

Charlie's face reddened as he leapt to her defence.

"Leave her alone, Flynn! It's not her fault if she has a heart."

Kitty smiled at him gratefully. Flynn spat on the ground.

"A soft heart at that! Soft hearts get people killed in this world."

The boy slipped away, disappearing silently into the streets. Kitty looked at Charlie.

"Why does he hate us so much?"

Charlie shrugged.

"Don't know. It's his problem as far as I'm concerned. As long as he doesn't take it out on you."

Kitty smiled again, grateful for his defensiveness, if a little embarrassed.

"Thanks Charlie, but I can look after myself you know."

"I know you can Kitty. I don't know many people who can stick up for themselves as well as you. I… I didn't mean to annoy you…"

He looked anxiously at Kitty's face. Kitty smiled at his concern and gave him a brief hug. His face cracked into a grin.

"You can stick up for me anytime."

The two friends sat quietly for a moment, neither sure what to say, neither wanting to break the moment. Suddenly Polly's brash voice rang in their ears.

"Don't you worry about Flynn. He's all right, just takes a while to get to know him."

Kitty considered that to be a great understatement, but did not comment.

"Anyway mates, we got some news. Come and listen to little Davey Jones here. He's got something to tell you."

She beckoned to a young boy who was hanging back away from them. He couldn't have been more than eight or nine. He was dressed in grimy grey wool with a cloth cap and a soot-blackened face. He smiled nervously at them.

"Come on then Davey, spit it out! We haven't got all day."

Polly pushed the lad gently into the centre of the small group. He looked slightly awed by the company. Suddenly, as if making up his mind, he stuck his chin out, with a hint of defiance.

"Them blokes you've been lookin' for, well I think I've found the other one. Tall, skinny, supposed to be a copper. Seems he's forgotten all about that now."

"Where is he? What's he doing?"

Davey grinned at the excitement in Kitty's voice.

"Last I saw him, he was in Spice Island – drinking. Left him there a little while ago. But I've been tailing him for ages. Never noticed me once he didn't. Could've tapped the idiot on the shoulder and he still wouldn't have seen me. Anyway you might want to know where he was going."

The boy paused, expectantly. Kitty and Charlie leaned in towards him, caught up in the intrigue. Polly sat back, surveying them all with amusement.

"Lumps Fort."

Kitty and Charlie looked confused.

The old fort, the other side of the Great Morass. There's not much there now. Just a semaphore station with a couple of old men running it. Hasn't been used as a fort in years. But it's being used for something. He goes over there a few times a day. Always on his own, but the semaphore men seem to know him. At least they always let him in. Sometimes he takes food with him. Not for him though." Davey laughed. "It's food, but it don't look that appetising. Even for a hungry lad like me."

He rubbed his stomach to emphasise his hunger and looked expectantly at Polly. Polly laughed.

"Don't worry Davey lad, we'll see your stomach is filled in a minute."

Charlie, Kitty and Polly looked at each other.

"Are you thinking what I'm thinking?" asked Charlie.

"Hmm. Might be worth a little visit, don't you think? See what he's up to."

Polly looked doubtful.

"Are you sure about this? Normally if I see coppers, I go the other way. Still, I suppose we could check it out. Davey, can you take us there? Tonight?"

She looked over at Davey, who once again rubbed his stomach pointedly. Polly sighed. "Of course, after you've had your dinner."

***

The man rubbed his bleeding wrists inside the manacles. He knew it was futile to continue. He would not break the metal with his bear arms. But he couldn't help himself trying. At least it took his mind off his captivity for a while. He rubbed a few times more, grunting in pain and frustration. Then his shoulders slumped, as the extent of his impotence hit him.

Jacob lay in the dark and thought. He thought of his family. He thought of the men who had betrayed him. And he thought of the English who had brought him to this god-forsaken land and incarcerated him like a beast.

Africa seemed a long time ago now. He could not say he missed it anymore. It was too intangible, too distant an idea. He had been a young man when he left, full of anger. Over the years, anger had given way to sadness, resentment turned to resignation. But he never forgot the injustice. The memory might fade, but he would not forget.

He missed the plantation. He would never have expected to. Sat in the foul-smelling chill of the dank tunnel he longed for the spicy heat of Jamaica. He longed for his small patch of land, carefully tended over the years. He wondered what had become of his plantains, his sweet potatoes, his yams, growing without him in the soil. He supposed that someone would have appropriated his garden. They would have to. Anything else would be a waste.

He missed his wife and children. He would always miss them. It was many years since he had seen them. He still remembered his daughter as a little baby: how the tiny hands would reach for his face as he looked down at her; how she would smile in recognition when he returned from his labours, innocently unaware of this world of cruelty and injustice. He remembered his sons, playing in the fields as he toiled, chasing the goat round the village, naked in the African sun, giggling with childhood abandon. He did not know what had become of them, if they were even alive. And he cried with the knowledge that he could never see them again.

Chapter 9

Kitty paused and looked back over the fields they had just crossed. In the distance she could see the lights of Croxton Town, pinpricks of white against the hill behind, mirroring the stars above them. She looked across to Portsea, her home, but it lay hidden, shrouded in the smog that enveloped the city. Somewhere in there were her parents. Somewhere in there was safety.

She shook her head. Nowhere was safe. Not now. They would have to carry on. There was no other choice. She looked at the fort, a low dark lump ahead of them. Above it, the tall semaphore mast was silhouetted against the indigo of the night sky, it's paddle like arms jutting out at ungainly angles.

"You're sure this is the right place?"

Polly's voice sounded almost cheerful.

"I ain't sure of anything. But this is what they reckon. Davey, you ain't leadin' us on a wild goose chase are you?"

The young boy puffed his chest out indignantly.

"Course I ain't. This is where he comes. Followed him myself I have. A few times now."

"Good lad. We'll give you a medal when we get back, or a penny if you're lucky. Now, how do we get in?"

The boy pointed and they squinted into the dark, trying to follow his finger.

"That's the main gate over there. There's a gatehouse just inside. That's where they live. There's two of them. They take it in turns to man the semaphore tower. From what I've seen, they're drunk most of the time, but it's still a risk. The man on the semaphore tower can see all round. That's the point really."

Polly clipped him playfully round the ear.

"Don't get too clever, mister. Or you may be getting too big for those boots of yours. Are you sure there's just the two of them?"

Davey nodded vigorously.

"Yes, definitely. I've watched them for a few days. Occasionally the copper comes to see them, but most of the time it's just the two of them."

"So, if we don't want to use the gate, how do we get in?"

The boy smiled, the white of his teeth catching the moonlight.

"Over there." He pointed again, to the western edge of the fort. "The wall's caved in for about twenty feet. It's a bit of a rough scramble, but the men never go there, and in the dark they shouldn't spot you. Once you're in, stick to the south wall. About a third of the way along there's a door that leads to the old rifleman's tunnel. That's where he goes, every day, the older man. He takes the food and water with him and comes out without it, every day."

Kitty interrupted excitedly.

"They're keeping someone in there. It's the only explanation."

Polly whistled softly.

"Well done Davey boy. Clever lad." She looked round at the others. "Who's up for a rescue mission then?"

They crept silently towards the western wall of the fort. As Davey had said, a section of the wall had tumbled down, leaving a rough slope of earth and brick. It wouldn't be too hard to climb, but they would have to be very careful not to make a noise, and just hope the man in the semaphore tower was too drunk or too asleep to notice. Just before they reached the wall they stopped.

"Alright Davey boy, this is as far as you come. Now beat it back home."

Polly's voice was kindly and she smiled as she spoke, but Davey could see the firmness in her eyes. He protested briefly, but she shook her head.

"No Davey, we're going on alone. It's going to be dangerous, this next bit. Besides, if we don't come back, someone needs to know where we've gone."

Davey nodded, and quietly slipped back into the night. They waited until he was gone before they turned their attention back to the wall and began to climb.

The climb was agonisingly slow. Every movement seemed sure to give them away. The slope was not steep, but the earth and rubble shifted under their weight. On two occasions Kitty had to stifle a cry as a lump of rock landed on her hand or foot, the rough granite digging into her flesh. About half-way up Charlie's foot slid under him, setting off a shower of stones down the slope. In the silence of the night the tiny landslide seemed deafeningly loud and the children froze where they were, terrified of discovery. After a few agonisingly long, but uneventful, minutes they started to move again, slowly, even more cautiously.

In the centre of the section of wall, a large gap had been formed by the collapse, creating an uneven 'V' shape. One by one they passed through the gap, and dropped the short distance into the courtyard beyond.

They crouched silently in the shadows below the wall, listening for any sounds of alarm. The quiet of the night was disturbed only by the hoot of an owl and the sudden scuffling of its prey in the grass. To the north a faint glow of light marked the gatehouse, where one or both of the watchmen were making best use of a flagon of ale to while away the hours. Slowly, cautiously they felt their way along the inside of the wall. The ground was rough underfoot, the flagstones cracked and overgrown, and liberally scattered in rubble from the wall above. A number of times they stopped and waited, hoping that they had not been discovered. All the time, the semaphore tower loomed above them, it's signal arms waving menacingly in the dark. Kitty felt terrifyingly exposed in the moonlit courtyard. At any moment she was sure that someone would look down and see them. But they didn't, and eventually they reached a doorway, set into the thick hill that formed the southern wall of the fort.

"This must be it." hissed Polly. Charlie nodded. Kitty could just about make out the grey shape of his head against the ebony blackness of the night.

Polly turned the handle carefully. The handle turned but the door didn't move. Tracing the door up and down with his hands Charlie found two large bolts securing the door in place. They were well oiled and easily glided silently back in their brackets. The door swung open, the creaking hinges sounding ominously loud in the silence of night. From behind the door a waft of stale air greeted their nostrils, and the mouth of a dark tunnel opened before them.

Polly led the way, followed by Kitty. Charlie carefully closed the door behind them, pulling it to but ensuring they could still push it open. Inside the tunnel it was pitch black. Kitty could not even make out the shape of Polly's head in front of her.

"We need some light." she whispered.

"I've got my tinder box," replied Charlie behind her, "wait a moment and I'll light a candle."

They heard the percussive grating of flint on metal and saw a shower of sparks fly from Charlie's hands. The candle caught, and the tiny flame grew and flickered, casting eerie shadows around them. They were in a long tunnel, the arched brick roof low above their heads. The walls around them were white with mould.

A soft groan sounded from ahead. The three children stopped, not daring to move. Kitty clenched her fists, wondering nervously what lay ahead. She peered into the gloom. The thin glow of the candlelight petered out quickly and she could see nothing beyond. Not daring to call out, she stepped carefully forwards. Polly followed her lead and they crept cautiously up the tunnel. Within thirty yards the tunnel opened out into a large square chamber. At the back of the chamber, staring up at them, eyes wide in surprise, sat a man, chained by his hands and feet. His clothes had once been fine but now were torn and dishevelled. His face was bruised and matted with dried blood. Despite the battered appearance, Kitty recognised the resemblance at once.

"George Pemberton?"

The man nodded.

"We're here to rescue you."

***

Joseph Chamberlain tapped the silver top of his black cane against the window of the coach. He smiled to himself. He was looking forward to the forthcoming confrontation. He knew, or guessed, much, but there were still answers he needed. They would move them tonight. The fort was becoming too dangerous. Portsmouth was becoming too dangerous. Too many people knew, or guessed too much.

Mr Moseley would help take care of everything. Mr Chamberlain had come to rely on the man's undemonstrative efficiency. As far as he could tell, Mr Moseley had a very limited repertoire of emotions, callous indifference being the most prominent. Unappealing though this may seem, it made him a most effective accomplice for Mr Chamberlain's machinations.

He had, of course arranged the despatch of Mr Samuelson with his trademark ruthlessness. The policeman had been losing his nerve. Joseph had recognised the signs. It would only have been a matter of time before he talked. Some people were motivated by greed, others by ambition. Mr Samuelson had been motivated by fear, and sooner or later his fear of the authorities would have overcome his fear of Mr Chamberlain. This was, of course, somewhat ironic, given the circumstances of his death. Some people were such poor judges of character.

The other policeman was more robust. Joseph was confident that self-interest would keep him quiet for the time being. At least as long as he was still useful. Nonetheless, he was still a loose end, and one that he would need Mr Moseley to tidy up in due course. Leave no trace behind. That would have been his motto, if he had really believed in mottoes. The girl troubled him though. He knew that he should also remove her and her friend, but unusually he found himself loathe to do so. He gently chided himself for his own squeamishness. Such sentiment would get him killed if he allowed himself to succumb to it.

The coach rattled on through the dark. He would move the men to his country estate. They would have more privacy there, in which to become truly acquainted. Mr Moseley and Mr Bartholomew would both accompany them. One could not be too secure in such a venture. This would also allow Mr Moseley to arrange for Mr Bartholomew to meet his unfortunate demise somewhere on the journey back to Portsmouth.

Mr Chamberlain smiled to himself again. The plan was all falling in to place. The earlier complications seemed to have been successfully eradicated, and after tonight there would be nothing left to link him to the whole sordid affair. They had one more stop, one more piece of the puzzle to pick up, and then it would be time for the final act to begin.

***

"Who are you?"

The man's voice was hoarse. With shouting, Kitty suspected. In this desolate fortress you could shout for days and no-one would hear you. The sound would be swallowed by the thick stone and earth of the ramparts, and all you would hear in reply would be the scuttling of rats and the steady drip of water in the damp passages.

"My name is Kitty, and this is Polly, and Charlie. We're friends of your son."

The man's damaged features came suddenly alive with excitement.

"Philip? You've seen Philip? Is he safe?"

"Yes. Don't worry Philip is safe. We promised him we would find you. And now we have so let's get you out of here."

Kitty looked uncertainly at the thick metal manacles, chaining the man's hands and feet to the wall, but Polly pulled from her pocket a small set of metal rods and wires. She grinned at Kitty.

"Lockpicks."

It took a few minutes of fiddling, but soon Polly had sprung open all the chains and the man was standing, a little unsteadily, rubbing his chafed and bloodied wrists. He looked at the children.

"I don't know how I can ever thank you."

"You can thank us later," replied Polly, "but right now the best thing we can do is get ourselves out of here."

She started to walk off, back down the tunnel, but the man called her back.

"Wait." Polly stopped. The man continued. "There is another prisoner here. We can't leave him. He… he's the reason they took me in the first place."

Polly looked mutinous.

"Hold on mister, we've risked enough already. Do you want to be caught again? If not we need to go. Quickly."

She started to move off again but the man called again.

"Wait. This man, he has been treated far worse than me. If we leave him they will kill him. If we leave him it will…, it will all have been for nothing."

His voice cracked as he spoke, but he looked up at Polly with clear eyes and said in a soft voice,

"My wife's death. It will have been for nothing."

Polly looked away from him and over at Kitty. Kitty felt more terrified than she had ever felt in her life. But as she looked at the man her fear was overwhelmed with sorrow - sorrow and a fervent desire to help. She looked beseechingly back at Polly.

Eventually Polly nodded.

"Come on then. Let's not hang around."

***

Once again they crept, quietly into the moonlit courtyard, their shadows flickering across the wall behind them. George Pemberton went ahead, looking around cautiously, as if adjusting to the openness around him. At one point the gatehouse door was flung open, spilling a blaze of light into the courtyard around it. They shrank back against the wall, willing the shadows to swallow them. A man appeared in the doorway. One hand held the doorframe, the other a tankard. He belched loudly into the night, then stepped back inside and shut the door. Kitty breathed a sigh of relief.

Pemberton pointed across the courtyard. Set in the opposite wall, beyond the gatehouse, they saw another door, firmly shut and bolted. "He's in there. At least he was when they brought me here. We can't just leave him." Polly nodded.

"If we go the long way round, along the side of the fort, I think we can make it. That way we stay in the shadows and we don't get too close to the gatehouse, or the tower."

They all looked up at the semaphore tower, looming above them. There was no sign of any occupancy, and Kitty hoped fervently that whoever was supposed to be up there was neglecting his duty for the evening.

When they arrived at the door they again found it bolted. The bolt was stiff and, as Pemberton forced it open, it flew back with a resounding clang. Kitty looked around her nervously, but nothing moved.

Through the door and into the corridor beyond, another tunnel stretched darkly into the earth ramparts. Cocooned in the dank brick catacomb, Kitty tried to shake off the sense of foreboding that suddenly threatened to overwhelm her. As Polly quietly pulled the door closed behind them, Charlie struck a light once again to the candle. The tiny flare of light cast flickering shadows around them, but Kitty was grateful for its warm glow. Slowly, cautiously they crept down the narrow tunnel. Once again it opened out at the end into a larger chamber. Once again they saw, chained and shackled to the wall, the figure of a man, curled into the corner of the chamber. As they approached, the man looked up. Kitty gasped. His face shone black in the flickering candlelight. A sheen of sweat reflected the flame. The right side of his face was swollen and puffy around the eye. But the eyes were clear and looked straight at Kitty, and the voice was softly confident.

"Ah. Who might you be? Not my captors that's for sure. Could it be that you've come to rescue me?"

* * *

Kitty stared at the man in amazement.

"What's the matter? Never seen a black man before?"

"Yes. I mean, no. I'm sorry. I didn't mean to stare."

The man laughed mirthlessly.

"Don't worry. I'm used to it."

George Pemberton fidgeted uncomfortably.

"This is Jacob. He's been their prisoner longer than I have. Polly, can you do the honours."

Polly grinned cheekily.

"Course I can. Hang on there matey, we'll have you free in no time."

Once again Polly stepped up and set to work. Her lock-picking skills were being put to good use that night, Kitty reflected. Kitty marvelled at the surety of her fingers as she deftly sprung the lock.

Jacob stood, stretching painfully as if he was learning the movements anew. His body was lean, almost stretched, and his face looked older and sadder than Kitty had expected from the voice. He looked seriously at Polly.

"Thank you girl. Thank you for loosing my chains."

He looked at his hands as if staring at them for the first time.

"If this is freedom, it may take me some time to get used to the taste."

"Your English is good, Mr er.. Mr…"

The man smiled.

"Jacob. You can call me Jacob. Yes my English is good. It is my fifth language, but I have had plenty of time to practise."

Kitty's mind reeled at the idea of speaking five languages. It was all she could do

sometimes to cope with the one she had.
While Kitty grappled with this concept,
Polly's voice cut sharply through the silence.
"I hate to break up the pleasantries folks, but
couldn't we do them some place else? I don't
know about you but I'm quite keen to be
getting out of here."
Jacob nodded.
"Not as keen as I am. Let us go quickly."
They made their way back up the
subterranean corridor. At the end they
reached the stout door to the courtyard. As
Charlie put his hand up to push against the
door they heard the grating of metal from the
other side of the door and then a sharp thud.
Charlie pushed against the door but it would
not budge.
"It's no good. I can't move it!"
With a sickening feeling in her stomach Kitty
realised what the sound had been.
"The bolt. Someone's pulled the bolt to.
We're trapped!"
George Pemberton and Jacob threw
themselves against the door with all their
weight. Three times they hurled their bodies
at the wooden panels, but the door stood,
immovably solid. After the third attempt they
stepped back, both breathing heavily in the
stale atmosphere of the tunnel. From beyond

the door came the sound of mocking laughter, followed by a coarse voice.

"Well, well, well! Look what little rats we've caught in our trap!"

George Pemberton mustered as much dignity as he could.

"Who are you sir? I demand that you open this door and show yourself."

"You, Mr Pemberton, are in no position to demand anything. I, on the other hand, am in a much stronger position. Of course I will open the door, but all in good time. After all, Mr Chamberlain will be so looking forward to meeting his guests."

Chapter 10

Kitty gasped and looked over at Charlie. His eyes widened slightly, but he looked steadily back at her with as confident a face as he could manage. It didn't quite convince her, but she took some comfort from his efforts.

"Well," she said, trying to sound more nonchalant than she felt, "at least we'll get to meet the mysterious Mr Chamberlain."

George Pemberton looked worried.

"He's not a man to be trifled with Kitty. Not a man I'd wish you to meet, especially under these circumstances."

Philip's words came back to Kitty.

"My father wasn't scared of anyone, but he was scared of Mr Chamberlain. He used to say he was the devil, and that if anything ever happened to him, then it would be the devil's work."

She shuddered, thankful for a moment for the dark that concealed her fear. She looked at George Pemberton.

"Do you fear him Mr Pemberton."

The man looked at her, squinting in the candlelight. He nodded his head.

"I fear what he is prepared to do. We all should fear what he might do. He is a man without a soul. Yes, I fear him. But he will not beat us easily. I promise you that. For now, though, all we can do is bide our time and wait for our opportunity."

They waited in the dark. At Jacob's suggestion they snuffed the candle out. Who knew when they may have need of it again? In the inky blackness time seemed to lose all meaning, and Kitty could no longer tell whether they had waited minutes, hours or days. The sounds around them seemed to magnify and ring in the chamber. Kitty could not tell if it was the scuffling of a rat or just one of her companions shifting in the dark. More than once she felt something brush over an arm or leg, and twitched where she sat. But she did not scream. Whatever horrors her mind imagined she would not scream.

Sat there, in the dark, not knowing what might befall them, she thought of Joshua. She pictured him, sitting with her mother, playing with one of the small wooden toys her father sometimes brought home. She could see her mother in detailed perfection, every line on her face etched out. Her brother was slightly blurred, and she realised with a sense of shock that she could not quite recall the detail. She tried to remember his face, but the closer she looked, the more hazey the picture became.

Somehow if she thought about Joshua she found herself less scared. Whatever befell them, it could be no worse than what had happened to him, and she told herself that if the worst should happen, at least she would see her little brother again. It was not much, but it helped.

She thought about her mother. She remembered her mother's raw grief at Joshua's death, and felt a stab of guilt and remorse at the prospect of causing her such pain again. She thought about how annoying she had found her mother's constant cosseting, and yearned with all her heart for another moment of such attention.

She thought about her father. She thought of his apparent strength, and realised the pain that he must be forever holding in. She thought of his small smile when he looked at her, and the way that he called her 'Kitty'. Somehow he managed to make the word sound special, even if she couldn't work out what was different about it. She longed to be wrapped in his strong arms once again.

And then she thought about where they were, and what was about to happen, and why they were here. And she needed to know.

"Jacob," her voice was at first tentative in the dark, then bolder, "Jacob, what happened? Why are you here? Who are you?"

There was silence for a moment, then a small shuffling of someone moving nearby. Jacob's voice replied, deep and resonating throughout the chamber.

"My name was not always Jacob. Once, in my own home country, I was Lamin. I was sold into slavery long ago in Africa. Sold like an animal and brought here to be a servant to the fine lords and ladies of your country. And here I am, chained in a dungeon instead."

***

Time slid slowly past. For the most part they were silent, each pre-occupied with their own thoughts. Occasionally one of them would move, breaking the silence with the scrape of stone on stone and the rustle of their clothes. Even more occasionally someone would speak, searching for human contact in the isolating, disorientating darkness. But conversation quickly lapsed, and quietness would descend, smothering their words.

Kitty thought desperately of escape. Would they rush their captors, fight their way to freedom? But in her heart she knew they did not have the strength to fight. And as time wore on she felt the cold and dark sapping her will, steadily and inexorably weakening her beyond resistance.

She imagined Mr Chamberlain, her mind building a monster, huge, brutish and belligerent, casting death and destruction around him. Try as she might to contain her fear, to ignore the machinations of her mind, she could feel the panic rising within her. She closed her eyes and thought hard of her mother, her father, of Charlie. Kitty reached a hand out in the dark, groping sightlessly against the rough stone floor. Her hand found another and held it. The warmth alone gave her some comfort. Somehow she knew it was his. She heard his whispered voice, close by her ear.

"Kitty?"

"Charlie."

"It'll be all right Kitty, just you see."

"I know."

She didn't, and from the wavering in his voice she knew he didn't either. But it was enough for both of them to believe for the time being. Eventually they heard the clinking of keys behind the door and the scraping of the bolt being prised back. Kitty felt Charlie tense,

and squeezed his hand in hers. The rough
voice called out,
"Stand back from the door. I have a pistol,
and the first person to come out will get a
bellyful of lead."
They didn't move. In the dark they sat,
waiting for the door to open. It took a few
moments but soon they heard the last bolt
sliding out and the creak of the hinges as the
door opened into the night. A lantern cast a
pool of light into the tunnel. In its glow,
leering unpleasantly at them, Kitty saw a
sallow, thin face, slightly pockmarked, with
hard, unsympathetic eyes. He looked at Kitty.
"You should have kept your nose out of
business that didn't concern you."
Kitty recognised him at once. He was the
taller one of the two policemen that had been
chasing them. Behind him another figure
stood, shrouded in shadow. She squinted into
the dark, but could see nothing other than the
murky grey of his silhouette. Behind her she
heard the rasp of George Pemberton's voice,
catching drily in his throat.
"Chamberlain."
She stared in fascinated horror, as the
shadowy figure emerged, his thin, angular
limbs solidifying in the lantern light. A flare
of flame suddenly illuminated his features and

she gasped as she looked into the smiling face of Mr Samuel Peabody.

"Mr... Mr Peabody. I don't understand."

"My rather vulgar friend is right Kitty. You really should have learnt to curb your inquisitiveness. Now, I am afraid, it is too late."

The smile remained, but the menace of the words rang clearly in the icy tone of his voice. George Pemberton rose to his feet. The policeman instantly raised his pistol, pointing it right at Pemberton's chest.

"Steady there, my friend. Wouldn't want anyone to get hurt now, would we?"

As if to reinforce his point, another man, short and thickset, appeared at the mouth of the tunnel, the dull metallic gleam of a pistol glinting in his hand.

Pemberton stopped, eyes glaring at the men.

"You won't get away with this, Chamberlain."

"My dear Pemberton, I think you'll find that I have got away with it. Oh, before you think of doing anything else foolish, you ought to know that I have something of yours, something oh so precious to you..."

Kitty's heart shrank with fear. She looked towards Pemberton, wishing she could stop time, go back and undo what she had done.

"Mr Pemberton, I'm so sorry. Mr Peabody…
we thought he was our friend. We trusted
him. We thought…"

A look of confusion passed over Pemberton's
face. He looked quizzically at Kitty, before
turning his attention back towards Peabody.
"Come on Philip, come on out, come and see
your father."

In an instant confusion turned to
comprehension, shock and anger. Then, as
quickly as it had flared, the anger faded.
Pemberton's face crumpled and his shoulders
sagged. Peabody turned and, from the
darkness behind him, he pulled a young boy
into the small pool of light.

"Philip!"

"Father!"

Pemberton started forward, but again the
muzzle of the pistol waved in his direction,
stopping him where he stood. Kitty caught a
slight movement from Mr Peabody out of the
corner of her eye and looked across at him.
To her horror she saw a long, but extremely
thin, blade appear in his hand. He held it to
Philip's throat and gently pulled the boy's
head back, as if caressing a much-loved son.
"Philip, meet my favourite stiletto knife. Its
blade is *exceptionally* sharp, I think you'll
agree. It's up to you now, Mr Pemberton.

You know what I want. You can either give it to me or watch as I ever so slowly, ever so carefully, dissect and disembowel your son in front of you. The choice is yours."

"And what will happen if I tell you?"

"Well, you will die of course. You know far too much to live. Besides which, a number of very powerful gentlemen have paid me an inordinately large sum of money to ensure that you do not live. So yes, I am afraid you will have to die."

George Pemberton looked on impassively and did not move.

"But Philip, well now, that is another matter. He is, after all, an extremely likeable boy, very much like his late, beautiful mother." Philip made a choking sound, and George Pemberton twitched, frustrated at his powerlessness.

"Ah yes, I was so sorry about what happened to her. Again, inevitable I am afraid. But such a waste! An amazing woman, your mother, Philip. Truly amazing."

"What will happen to Philip?"

"He will live with me. As my adopted son. He will want for nothing. He will be brought up with all that money can buy, and eventually, I will find him a suitable heiress to marry. If you tell me what I need to know!"

Again the threat hung, heavy in the air. George Pemberton looked to the floor. He looked up again, his pained eyes meeting his son's.

"Father, please…"

A look of agony passed over Pemberton's face. He looked again at Peabody and shrugged his shoulders.

"All right."

Suddenly Jacob's voice boomed out from the darkness of the tunnel.

"And what about the other children?"

Peabody turned in the direction of the voice.

"Ah Jacob. How nice to make your acquaintance once again. You have been, may I say, a much sought after man."

"What about the other children?"

"They are, I am afraid to say, expendable, and will therefore need to be disposed of."

It took Kitty a moment to comprehend the enormity of his words.

"No! How can you say that! We tried to help you!"

At her hiss of shock, Peabody tutted quietly.

"I am sorry my dear Kitty. I really am. After all, you are a remarkably resourceful young lady. I could take you on as well if you wanted. You could be my apprentice. I would teach you everything. Eventually

Philip and you could share my empire."

"And Charlie? And Polly?"

"Alas, there is never room for everybody. Just you and Philip I am afraid. You would have to leave Charlie and Polly behind."

The words were followed by an ominous pause. Eventually Kitty spoke.

"Never. I'd rather die."

"Very well. That, of course, is the other option. We shall see to it later." He turned back to Pemberton. "Now Mr Pemberton. The location of the papers please, or I will decide which part of your son's anatomy to remove first."

As if to prove the point, he let the blade of his stiletto pierce the taut skin of Philip's throat. A tiny sliver of blood welled on Philip's neck and ran down towards his collar. Philip didn't move.

"There, there, brave boy," murmured Peabody, "I'm sure your father will see reason."

George Pemberton stood, as if making the words to reply, but finding them stuck in his throat. He tried to speak once, twice, still the words would not come.

"Tell him." It was Jacob's voice. "Tell him, and it will all be over."

Again Pemberton tried to speak. Peabody's stiletto carved a slightly longer trace of red along Philip's throat.

"Need some more encouragement Pemberton? Let me see now, how would you like… an ear… an eyeball…" the stiletto hovered in front of the boy's eyes, "… maybe a finger… or just a lock of hair?"

A sudden swish of the blade and a large clump of Philip's hair fell to the floor.

"Let us see, where shall we begin?"

A desperate groan escaped Pemberton's lips, but before he could answer there was a crash, a burst of flame and a sudden cacophony of yelling voices. Kitty's head whirled with the chaos. Fire licked at the sides of the tunnel and black smoke billowed around them. A second flash and a sharp retort sounded, close to Kitty's ears, leaving her slightly deafened with a high pitched whine in the background. She heard a grunt of pain behind her, and a hand grabbed hers pulling her forwards off balance. Kitty put her head down and ran.

Chapter 11

Out in the fresh night air Kitty turned and looked back behind her. The mouth of the tunnel was obscured by smoke pouring out of it. Outside the tunnel a number of people seemed to be wrestling each other. One of them Kitty recognised as the burly, thick-set figure of their erstwhile captor. The other three or four were smaller, child-sized. Nowhere could she see Mr Peabody or Philip.

"Philip!" shouted Kitty in alarm, "Where is he?"

"Polly!" shouted Charlie, his hand still gripping hers.

Charlie loosed his grip on her hand and dived back into the smoke.

"Charlie, no!" shouted Kitty, but he was gone. A moment later another dark figure swept past her into the tunnel. With a momentary thrill of shock, she recognised the slight frame of Flynn. She took a deep breath and ran back in.

Inside the tunnel was pitch black, the smoke stinging her eyes. She ducked her head down to stay beneath the worst of the smoke and her hands found a body, lying on the floor. She could not tell who it was, but she shook hard, hoping against hope for some sign of life. The body remained motionless and she pulled hard, trying to drag the person out of the tunnel, out of danger. Her limbs felt weak with exhaustion. She pulled again. There was some movement but not enough. Inch by inch she heaved her burden back, slowly, too slowly. The tunnel entrance seemed impossibly far away, unreachable. Her lungs were bursting, straining, drained of that one long breath that seemed so long ago. Kitty knew she must not breathe again. One breath of that thick black smoke would be the end of her. But it seemed so hard, so foolish not to. She felt herself drifting, waiting to settle by the body she carried, not letting go, but no longer moving. She felt herself start to take one searing, stinging breath.

And then she felt hands grabbing her, wrenching the body from her, pulling her free into the starlight. She felt herself collapse onto the cold cobbles, coughing and retching onto the floor. The blood rushed in her ears and she fought for a few moments to breathe. When she sat shakily up, she saw Flynn, Polly and Charlie gathered anxiously around her.

"Kitty? Are you all right?"

She smiled weakly up at Charlie.

"Yes Charlie, I'll live. Thank you all for rescuing me."

It was Polly who replied.

"You'd done all the hard work yourself girl. You were practically at the entrance. If it wasn't for you he would still be in there."

Kitty looked down at the man lying on the floor where Polly pointed. George Pemberton was lying motionless on his side.

"Is he… is he alive?"

Polly nodded.

"Yes, he's alive. Badly wounded but alive. I think he'll survive but he needs help."

A commotion sounded at the mouth of the tunnel and the four children turned to stare. Out of the tunnel staggered Jacob. He was covered in smoke and blood, and reeled from side to side like a drunken man. Reaching the wall, he put a hand up to steady himself. He looked up at Kitty grimly.

"That's one of them won't be coming out of there."

It took Kitty a moment to understand what he meant.

"You've… you've killed him? Mr Peabody?"

Jacob shook his head.

"No. The other one. The one with the pistol." he grunted.

Kitty looked around the small courtyard, memory flooding back to her. She saw the three children Flynn had brought with him. One of them was young Davey Jones. She didn't recognise the other two. They were standing over a body on the floor. The body was short and squat, and the face deeply pockmarked. He did not look in the least like Peabody. She could not see Philip anywhere. "What about Philip? Where is he? And Mr Peabody?"

The others looked around them, blankly. Kitty's stomach turned in guilt and frustration. She had brought Philip to Peabody. She had given him to the very enemy he had been trying to escape. It was Flynn who came to her aid.

"I know where he'll be going. Davey, Billy, Meg! Look after that one." He gestured towards George Pemberton, still lying on the ground. "The rest of you, follow me!"

He raced through the courtyard towards the main gatehouse, closely followed by Kitty, Charlie, Polly and Jacob. The gatehouse door was open, the glow of the brazier spilling out into the night. Beyond the main gate stood a coach, oddly angled and without any horses.

"Found this on our way here," said Flynn cheerily, "thought it might be a good idea if we let the horses go for a run."

Kitty noticed that one of the cartwheels was twisted at a crooked angle, with several of the spokes broken. She looked at Flynn.

"Your handiwork?" she asked.

"Just for good measure." he replied with a grin. He pointed across the fields, squinting into the distance. Kitty followed his hand. It was hard to make anything out in the gloom, and Kitty couldn't help but be impressed by Flynn's eyesight. Gradually as she stared, two figures became apparent, small moving shapes, a slightly different colour of dark. They chased after the shapes, Flynn leading, through the waterlogged meadow. The ground was soft and boggy underfoot, and their progress seemed frustratingly slow. After a few minutes Kitty looked up. The shapes they chased seemed larger and more distinct. Their progress may have been slow, but their quarry was slower still. Kitty's spirits lifted, and a new burst of energy flooded through her. Her companions had noticed too, and they picked their pace up. It didn't take long before they could clearly see Philip and Peabody ahead of them. They were moving, but slowly. The land was increasingly marshy and often they would have to wade through muddy water up to their thighs. Philip, it seemed, was doing his best to sabotage Peabody's escape. His hands were bound, and Kitty could see Peabody's glinting stiletto waving dangerously. But still, Peabody was having to push the boy on, as Philip lingered, moving as ponderously as he dared.

"Well done Philip! You're not making it easy for him." Kitty murmured. Flynn flashed her a smile, that surprised and delighted Kitty. "Come on! We've got him now!"

Philip looked behind him, his face lifting in hope as he saw the pursuers. Peabody also turned and grasped Philip firmly, once again bringing the stiletto to his throat.

"Stop there! Any closer and I cut the boy's throat wide open."

Jacob produced the pistol that he had wrestled from his captor. Raising it, he levelled it carefully at Peabody's face.

"I wish the boy no harm, Peabody, Chamberlain or whatever your name is. But I will gladly blow your brains out and risk the consequences. Now let him go before I shoot."

Philip blanched at Jacob's words but made no movement or sound. He was chest deep in the watery marsh and, it seemed to Kitty, was very slowly sinking. Peabody, with his greater height, was up to his waist. He smiled at Jacob.

"Well my friend, it seems that we have reached a pretty impasse, haven't we? The question is this: Who should one believe? Am I to believe that you will shoot me, knowing that you risk harming the boy? Or are you to believe that I might slit the boy's throat, knowing that it will inevitably lead to my own destruction?"

They stood facing each other, in the pitch dark with the wind blowing hard across the plain from the south west. The cocking of Jacob's pistol sounded ominously loud in the silence. Jacob's finger whitened on the trigger and he closed one eye as he focused on his target. Mr Peabody smiled and dropped his hands to his side.

"It seems you have me sir. No need to shoot me, though I have no doubt you would happily do so if I gave you a reason. The boy is yours and I will come, as they say, quietly."

As the knife dropped from his throat Philip lunged away from Peabody and began to wade, clumsily through the swamp, towards the others. Jacob did not lower the pistol. His face contorted with inner struggle and his finger remained tight on the trigger. Peabody stood absolutely still, smiling serenely at the party before him. Kitty found herself holding her breath. She wanted to say something, to urge Jacob to lower his weapon, but she was terrified that if she broke the silence he would fire. They watched, frightened but intrigued, as anger wrestled with moderation across Jacob's face. Eventually, slowly, breathing hard, Jacob lowered the pistol.

"I will not kill you, though you would not do me the same courtesy. But I will watch you tried for your crimes sir. Now before I let you out of this swamp, you will drop that dainty knife of yours into the morass. Then you will step slowly this way and I will take you back to face justice."

Mr Peabody raised an arm to one side and carefully dropped his knife into the swamp. He strode through the thick, muddy water towards them until Jacob once again waved his pistol.

"Stop! That's far enough. Now stay there while I bind your hands."

He passed the pistol to Polly who took it nervously and held it up towards Peabody.

"If he tries anything, shoot him. Don't worry about hitting me. Just shoot him and be done with it."

Polly nodded, looking unconvinced. Jacob unbound Philip's hands and carried the cords across to Peabody. He grabbed Peabody's arms and pulled them roughly behind his back. As he did so Peabody appeared to fall off balance and Jacob reached out a hand to steady him. In a blur of movement, Peabody spun around, the glint of a blade appearing miraculously in his hand. As if in slow motion Kitty saw the blade slice through the air, heard Jacob's grunt of pain as he slid to his knees in the swamp. Then all sound was obliterated by the deafening retort of the pistol in Polly's hand.

Peabody leapt from Jacob's side and, reaching firmer ground, raced into the night. Flynn made to chase him, but his legs had settled into the mud that surrounded him, and slowed him down. Charlie and Kitty were less encumbered and followed him into the darkness. They had not made it far before they realised that their quarry had vanished. Already they were beginning to lose their sense of direction and Kitty worried that they wouldn't be able to safely find their way back. She looked at Charlie. It was hard to make his face out in the dark but she could sense his anxiety. She touched his arm gently.

"We've lost him. Come on, let's get back."
"But he must be here. We can't just give up.
We've got to keep looking for him."
Kitty squeezed his arm again.
"We've lost him. Let him go."

***

They retraced their steps carefully, back into
the morass where they had left the others.
When they arrived, they found Polly
bandaging Jacob's shoulder with strips of
Flynn's shirt. Flynn looked questioningly at
them as they returned. Kitty grimaced in
reply.
"We lost him. He disappeared before we got
far. There's no chance of finding him now.
How's Jacob?"
Jacob answered.
"I am not hurt too badly, thank you. The
knife cut quite deeply into my right shoulder
but did not damage anything too vital."
"That was lucky," burst out Charlie, "I was
worried he had killed you."
Jacob smiled.
"No, I am fortunate to be alive. But I don't
believe he wanted to kill me. He is very
skilled with a knife, and if he had wanted to

kill me, I doubt I would be here now. I don't know why, but it seems I have been spared." He frowned a little.

"You are lucky you didn't find him. He is a dangerous man. I hate to think what would have happened if you had cornered him."

Kitty began to protest, but stopped, realising the truth in his words.

"I should have been more careful though. I knew he was dangerous. I should have guessed he had another knife. A man like him does not give up as easily as that. Come. Help me up. Let us see how the boy's father fares."

***

Joseph Chamberlain lay in the dark and listened, waiting until all sounds of the children had disappeared. They had run straight past him, their legs sloshing through the watery reeds in which he was concealed, his mud-covered features blending into the surrounding foliage. He remained still as they returned, walking this time more sedately back to their friends.

He was not concerned about capture. Had he needed to, he would not have struggled to despatch them both, dropping their bodies into the cold bog. He was confident in that. The only real threat had been Jacob, but he had seen to him. The shoulder wound would not kill Jacob, but it would weaken him for a while.

No, it was not fear that kept him hidden, covered in mud and water, only enough of his face showing to breathe and to see. It was, and he was most surprised to discover this in himself, a sensation almost bordering on compassion. He did not wish to shed any more blood tonight, particularly that of the children. He had shocked himself by his impulsive decision to spare Jacob's life. In other circumstances such mercy may have got him killed. But having done so, he had to admit to a certain satisfaction. He did not want to ruin it by taking such young lives unnecessarily.

He would have liked to say a few words to Kitty before he left. He had been right. She was bright, very bright, and she would go far. But for now he would have to leave her, to go back to her own.

He could hear the party of people, wading away from him, the splashing of legs and arms mingling with the subdued hum of voices. He lay still until all sound had ceased, then disappeared into the night.

***

Back at the fort all was quiet. Flynn's companions were guarding the remaining erstwhile captor with a zeal that bordered on enjoyment. Possibly a little too much enjoyment thought Kitty, as she watched one of the children nudge the prone body rather over-enthusiastically with a heavy looking leather boot.

Smoke continued to billow from the rifleman's tunnel, but the fire had failed to spread, held in check by the days of rain that had saturated the solid earthwork walls.

George Pemberton was awake, and sat upright, leaning against a stone pillar, his face pale, his breath coming fast and shallow.

Philip rushed over to him.

"Father! Father! Will you be all right?"

George Pemberton looked up at his son and smiled weakly.

"Philip, thank the lord, you are safe. I will be all right now."

He held Philip in a close embrace, the boy's head against his chest. Looking over the muddy mop of his son's hair, his eyes met Jacob's.

"Thank you Jacob."

"It is I who should be thanking you."

Polly looked across at Flynn.

"Anyway, what were you doing, interfering in my business? I had it all covered."

Flynn snorted, and his mouth twisted in a cheeky grin.

"Oh, I just figured you and your friends could do with a little help. Sorry if I ruined your carefully laid plans."

Kitty looked over nervously. She was still a bit unsure of herself with Flynn, but without him – well, she shuddered to think what might have happened.

"Thank you, Flynn. Thank you for rescuing us."

Flynn looked for a moment as if he was going to make some sharp comment in reply. Then his face relaxed, and he smiled into Kitty's eyes.

"It's a pleasure. You know Kitty, I've changed my mind about you. You're all right."

He held out a mud-encrusted hand. Kitty took it, and returned his smile.

Chapter 12

Kitty and Charlie approached the steps of the large terraced house with some trepidation. She thought of the last time she had knocked on such a door and resisted the temptation to run around to the back entrance. Mr Pemberton had been very clear. Eleven o'clock in the morning, number forty-three Hampshire terrace. The two friends were almost unrecognisable from the bedraggled urchins that had stumbled, exhausted from Lumps Fort two nights ago. Two nights seemed an age away, as they stood on the doorstep, scrubbed clean, in the smartest clothes that Kitty's mother had been able to gather together for them both.

"You'll need to look good for them fine folk now Kitty. And Charlie too. I've got some of Mrs Green's smart clothes, the ones her boy wore for his Pa's funeral. I'll give them a wash and a stitch and they'll be good as new."

She had kept her word as well. They did look as good as new. And Charlie looked both proud and a little self-conscious, as he shifted from foot to foot, trying to get comfortable in his recently acquired outfit.

A few moments later the door opened. To Kitty's surprise it was Mr Pemberton himself. He looked much better in a smart three-piece suit, although Kitty thought he still looked a little pale. He smiled at the two children. "Ah, you are here. And right on time too. Come on in please. There are a few people who are dying to see you."

Mr Pemberton turned and shuffled lopsidedly back into the house. Kitty noticed that he winced every time he twisted his body. He led them into the most spacious hall that Kitty had ever set foot in. She looked up at the chandeliers hanging above them and gasped at their height. Ahead of them a staircase, at least four times as wide as the staircase in Kitty's house, swept up to the next floor. Mr Pemberton walked past the staircase and then turned off into a side room. Kitty and Charlie followed.

The room they entered was of similar proportions to the entrance hall. In the opposite wall a large chimney breast housed a fire that roared and crackled merrily in the grate. Large leather chairs stood either side of the fire and Kitty's heart leapt as she saw Philip and Jacob occupying two of them. Jacob stood to greet them.

"The heroes of the hour! I have a lot to thank you for."

Philip ran forward and threw his arms around the pair of them, hugging them fiercely. In the corner of the room stood another man, one she didn't recognise. He was young and clean-shaven, with a mop of wiry hair, tightly curling around his forehead. He wore a velvet jacket and a dark cravat, but what impressed Kitty most was the inescapable energy that burned from his sharp eyes, as if he could barely contain the ideas that were bursting to escape. The strange young man stood up. His voice, when he spoke, was rich and resonant, and filled Kitty with the excitement that she had seen in his eyes.

"Yes, Jacob has much to thank you for. We all have much to thank you for. Our country has much to thank you for. You are a most exceptional pair of individuals!"

Mr Pemberton gestured towards the man, with a twirling flourish of his hand.

"Kitty, Charlie, may I present Mr Dickens."

Kitty curtseyed demurely, blushing scarlet as she did so. She was not sure if it was the formality of the occasion or the energy of Mr Dickens that made her blush. Charlie twisted his hands together and looked at the floor in discomfort, until, prodded sharply by Kitty's elbow, he managed a small, stiff bow.

Mr Dickens laughed, a deep, friendly laugh that instantly eased the tension in the room. "I must commend you both on your manners. But please, let us not stand on formality. Do call me Charles. Come we have much to discuss. It is because of you that this man, Jacob, has regained his liberty. You may not realise it, but you have helped uncover a scandal of most nefarious proportions."

Charlie wasn't sure what 'nefarious proportions' meant, but it sounded impressive. He and Kitty looked towards Jacob.

"I was born in Africa, but as a young man, I was captured and enslaved by British merchants. We were shipped out to Jamaica, crossing the heaving ocean in the stinking, rat-infested hold of a British ship. If you complained you were beaten. If you got sick, you died. But I was lucky. I survived. When we arrived in Jamaica I was stripped naked and sold at auction, sold to the highest bidder."

Jacob paused, but nobody spoke.

"I was sold to a sugar plantation. For years I worked in the fields, harvesting the sugar cane in the sweltering heat. That did not trouble me. I was used to hard work and I was used to the heat. But every day I worked, I thought of my wife and children. Every night as I slept, I dreamt of them.

Eventually, after I had been there several years, I was chosen to be a house-servant to my master. The work was much easier. I moved from my little hut on the plantation, to the grand house. I was smartly clothed, well-fed, but still I dreamed of my family."

"So how did you come to be here?" Charlie's eyes were wide, as he hung on Jacob's every word.

"My master was coming to visit England. Things had turned ugly in Jamaica, and he wanted to set up some business with a group of gentlemen in London. He decided to bring me with him. During my service, I had learnt not only the English language, but Dutch and French. I had, you might say, a natural aptitude. I was very useful to my master who spoke only English. I would accompany him to his meetings with Dutch and French businessmen, and later I would relay to him the things that they hadn't wanted him to hear."

"So, if you were so useful to him, how did you come to be chained and imprisoned in Lumps Fort?"

"Ah, Charlie. It is a good question you ask. Why was I not content to live in privileged slavery? Why was I not grateful for my fortune in being plucked from the cane fields? Well, despite all my luxuries, my fine clothes, my good food, I still did not have the two things I desired: my freedom and my family. I still remembered, you see. I remembered being my own person, farming my own land, raising my own children. Always I carried this with me, the desire to escape, to be once again a free person. And then, one fateful day, I met with Mrs Pemberton."

Jacob paused. He looked over at Philip. Philip returned his glance and nodded.

"It's all right. You can carry on. I would like you to tell the story."

"We travelled, my Master and I, to Chattersley House. It was another meeting, full of fine gentlemen, discussing ways of making money in order to become even finer gentlemen. The lady of the house was Mrs Pemberton, Eliza, Philip's mother and George's wife."

Philip blinked hard. His mouth twisted slightly at the corner, but he kept his head high, looking resolutely at Jacob.

"Eliza was different. Right from the start she treated me as a person, not merely an expensive chattel. She was fascinated by my languages, and talked to me of all the things I could do, if I was not a slave. At first I thought she was teasing me, but gradually it became clear that she was serious, and I began to really believe, for the first time, that I could break free, start a new life."

This time it was Kitty who spoke.

"So what happened?"

Jacob laughed sadly and looked away. Mr Pemberton took over the story.

"My wife, Philip's mother was the bravest woman I ever knew. And next to her, was Jacob, also risking not only his freedom but his life."

Mr Pemberton walked painfully across to his son and put an arm on his shoulder.

"Never forget that, Philip. Your mother was not only beautiful but so, so brave."

Philip looked up at his father. His voice was hushed, almost a whisper, and Kitty and Charlie leaned forward to hear.

"Why father? What did she do?"

Mr Pemberton paused. His face twisted, as if in pain. Then he continued.

"The story begins further back. Long before we met Jacob. Your mother was always a good woman. A woman of ideals and passion. Far more so than me. When she believed something she really believed it. Me? I merely followed where she led. They say that slavery was outlawed back in 1807, and yet here we sit with living proof of its existence. Your mother cared about a great deal of things, but few more than this. So the law changed but the slavers didn't stop. They just got cleverer and more cunning. Some people, your mother included, tried to stop them, tried to bring them to justice. In the end it was… it was something she gave her life for."

He broke off, swallowing hard. Philip looked determinedly at the floor. Kitty could feel her own eyes prickling and shining with tears.

"Why did they kill her?" she whispered, her throat feeling unusually tight.

"Eliza was not only brave, she was inquisitive." Pemberton smiled at Kitty. "They're both qualities she shared with a certain other young lady." Kitty blushed. "She asked questions, questions that people didn't want answered. She dug up secrets and pulled them apart. She wanted the world to know the terrible things that Britain was involved in. And eventually she stumbled on something - something scandalous, something sensational: a society so secret that it didn't even exist, full of people so important that nothing could touch them."

For Kitty it felt as if suddenly everything began to drop into place. In a breathy whisper she gasped,

"The Scarlet Order."

Pemberton nodded.

"Yes Kitty, the Scarlet Order. A secret order full of the most important people - pillars of society you might say. But they were pillars of society with distinctly shady foundations. No-one knows when the order started. Probably after the abolition of slavery in 1807. British slavers were still practising their terrible trade in Africa and the Carribean, but back home in England their wealthy lords and masters realised that they could no longer be associated with such illegal activity. They formed the Scarlet Order so that they could operate in secret, banding together in their evil endeavours. Well Eliza found out about them. But she needed to infiltrate them, to gather evidence to prove their corrupt dealings. And that's where I came in."

Kitty and Charlie looked puzzled.

"As a woman, Eliza would never be accepted into the order. She knew that, and enlisted my help. Eliza was well liked in society and it didn't take her long to find someone who would introduce me to the order. The idea was that I would help her to gather evidence, to bring down the order from inside."

"You were taking quite a risk yourself, sir!" exclaimed Charlie. Pemberton did not disagree with him.

"Yes. I suppose I was. But no more than my Eliza. Anyway, I joined the order, and we quickly realised how dangerous it was. The corruption ran far deeper than anyone would have imagined – right through the top of echelons of society. I was scared, I don't mind telling you. The people I was mixed up with were important, very powerful, and I knew that they would stop at nothing to keep their secrets hidden. Eliza knew that too but she was fearless, and never once wavered in her determination to put an end to their foul business."

"Who were they? Who were these people who were so important?"

Pemberton shrugged his shoulders helplessly. "Businessmen, government ministers, even priests. Every important institution was implicated. I knew who these men were, and I feared what they could do, but I tried my best. With Eliza's encouragement I spied and I listened, but I couldn't get any evidence. I wasn't part of the inner circle, wasn't close enough to the centre. Having newly joined I wasn't trusted with any of the Order's deeper secrets, and we knew we needed absolute proof if we were to have a hope of bringing any of them to justice. As the months wore on we began to despair. And then we met Jacob."

Kitty's eyes widened and she stared over at Jacob.

"George was not one of the inner circle, but my master was. He was at every meeting, every discussion, every deal or decision that was made. And as his servant, I went with him. Hah! How the irony of it never occurred to them. My master trusted me, he relied on me. But still, I remembered. I remembered what they did to me. I remembered the family they had taken from me. When Eliza came to me I knew this was my chance. I gladly agreed to help her. For months, I would feed her information, smuggling her the innermost secrets of the order. She would arrange for us to meet, passing messages through her husband. Soon she knew the full extent of the order's crimes, the full horror of their villainy. But she could do nothing without proof. She needed documents, signatures, evidence that no-one could deny, and eventually that was what I got for her."

Again Pemberton took up the tale.

"Jacob got what I couldn't, but at great risk to himself. His master was embroiled at the deepest level in the order's affairs, up to his neck in deals that would make your blood run cold. And Jacob knew about all of it. He was there when they made their deals. He was there when they signed their secrets away. And they never once suspected him."

"A slave. That's how they saw me. And who would trouble to keep secrets from an uneducated slave? I watched them as they drew up their documents, so arrogant in their own power, until eventually I seized my chance. My master was involved in the drawing up of a great treaty, between merchants of different countries, and involving some of the most powerful people in England. They planned to take a vast shipment of slaves out of Africa, to sell across the world. They had used their wealth and influence, bribing, lying and threatening, to persuade African rulers to turn a blind eye while they pillaged and enslaved African people. When I think of the burned homes, the children torn from their mothers, the families ripped apart, I am sick to my stomach."

Jacob stopped, his head bowed, his eyes burning.

"Jacob was entrusted by his master with a set of documents, papers which named and implicated all those involved in this abominable deal. He was to take it to the Grand Master…"

Kitty and Charlie looked perplexed. Pemberton continued.

"I know, it's a most peculiar title isn't it. The Grand Master was the head of the Scarlet Order. Incredibly pompous really, but powerful people love their titles. And Jacob was given the papers to take to him. Instead, he brought them to us.

It was beyond brave. It was beyond risky. Until then they had not suspected him. But with the papers gone, they would know what he had done, and the consequences didn't bear thinking about. These papers were just what we needed: conclusive proof, beyond all doubt, of the ringleaders' dirty involvement in the evil and illegal slave trade. Jacob knew how important it was, and he knew the risks. When he passed us the papers, we knew he couldn't go back. We knew we had to hide him, to help him escape, and we tried our hardest to do so. We arranged passage for him, on a ship from Portsmouth. We thought he would be safe but… but we were wrong." Pemberton broke off for a moment, choking back tears. Eventually he composed himself. "As it turned out they were watching us, just as we were watching them. There was a man in the order whose name I had come to know and fear. I knew him as Joseph Chamberlain. He was, unlike many of the others, not given to talking about his private life outside the order, so I knew little about him. But every plot, every plan, every evil deed that the order committed had him at the centre. I believe that he suspected us all along. He tracked down Jacob and captured him shortly before his ship sailed."

Kitty gasped and looked at Jacob.

"So you… you were the man in the sack, that night at the Spur Redoubt?"

Jacob nodded.

"Yes, that was me. I was betrayed by some of the sailors. The night before we sailed I was dragged roughly from my bed. I tried to shout for help but they gagged and bound me, and thrust a sack over my head. The rest you know."

Kitty and Charlie had listened, enthralled, to the story. Kitty was still bursting with questions. She turned back to George Pemberton.

"What happened to you? How did you come to be captured in the fort?"

"They took me first. They had never trusted me, I realise that now. I tried to carry on, to brazen it out. I realised that if I acted suspiciously that would only bring greater danger to Eliza and Jacob. The day after Jacob left I attended the order meeting in London, as usual. As soon as I arrived they were waiting for me and I knew that I was a prisoner. They were all there, all the leaders of the lodge. But the one that did the dirty work was Chamberlain."

His brow furrowed as he continued.

"They captured me and brought me down to Portsmouth. My captors at the fort were careless though. I caught a glimpse of Jacob as they brought him to his cell, and that was enough for me to guess what had happened. I knew Eliza would flee to Portsmouth with Philip. That much we had arranged in advance. But I didn't know what had befallen her, and I was terrified, alas with good reason. But then he had one piece of misfortune. He lost Eliza. He sent his spies out to find her. Well they found her, they murdered her and the rest you know. They would have killed me, I'm pretty sure, but I had one thing they needed, and for that they kept me alive."

Kitty nodded.

"The papers."

"Yes, the papers. You see Chamberlain and his henchmen had made a mistake. They killed Eliza without knowing what had become of the papers. The precious papers that proved their crimes."

"And where are the papers?"

"Well that is where I come in!"

The deeply resonant voice of Charles Dickens sounded from the corner, cutting across Kitty and Pemberton. Until then he had seemed content to linger in the background, but suddenly his presence filled the room. All heads turned to face him.

"Mr Dickens is a newspaper reporter. It was Mr Dickens that Eliza came to Portsmouth to meet." explained Mr Pemberton.

Charles Dickens nodded slowly.

"Yes, Eliza came to me. She wanted to entrust the whereabouts of the papers to me so that I could publish them in my newspaper and expose this scandal, but alas she died before she had the chance."

"So it was all for nothing. My mother died for nothing."

Philip's voice was flat, empty, soulless; his

face expressionless. Charles Dickens' face softened as he looked at Philip.

"No Philip. It was not for nothing. Fighting injustice is never for nothing. Your mother's sacrifice is tragic and terrible, but still for something she really believed in. You should always be proud of her. Before she died she hid the papers beyond the reach of Chamberlain and his associates. Only your father knew where they were hidden, and this is why they took him: to threaten and torture him into revealing their whereabouts."

Pemberton frowned.

"And who knows, I may have told them eventually. For myself, I would have endured anything. But they had Philip, and I could not bear to see them harm him. I would have talked."

"But father you didn't talk. And thanks to Kitty we are free! So are the papers still safe? Where are they?"

"The papers are safe. They were placed in a deposit box, in a bank in London, as soon as Jacob brought them to us. We knew their importance and the danger we were in."

Philip looked alarmed.

"Then we are still in danger! We must get to the papers, before the order find them... or us."

Charles Dickens smiled at Philip.

"Do not fear, young sir. You are all safe. The papers are in the hands of the magistrates in London. Warrants have already been issued for the arrests of Mr Samuel Peabody and the ringleaders in the Scarlet Order. At this very moment, my newspaper is publishing their shocking revelations for all to see. The power of the order is broken. Thanks to you a great scandal has been uncovered, and a great evil has been stopped."

Mr Pemberton paused, smiling sadly, and turned to Kitty.

"And now, young lady, I believe you have something of mine."

For a moment Kitty was confused, and stared blankly back at him. Then realisation dawned.

"You mean this?"

Kitty passed him the small twist of scarlet ribbon that she had taken from the body of his wife.

"Yes Kitty. This small piece of ribbon that symbolised a ruthless organisation of terror. Here, Sir, Eliza meant to give it to you. It may be of use in bringing these scoundrels to justice."

Charles Dickens closed his hand over the tiny

ribbon, a flicker of scarlet that disappeared in a moment.

Chapter 13

Lord Chief Justice[3] Augustus Walpole eased his over-sized stomach from behind the judicial bench and, standing somewhat stiffly, began to collect his papers. The dispensing of the King's justice was a tiring business.
He nodded to the clerk, who bustled around the courtroom with ostentatious efficiency, removing the evidence of a day's legal labour. Lord Walpole smiled to himself at the thought of the meal he would consume on his way home. The moral complexities of his recent judgement weighed no more on his mind than the welfare of the rats in the sewers. No man was above the law, of that he was sure. Outside the courtroom, the smell of wood polish mingled with the sweat and grime of the public. Lord Walpole raised a heavily scented handkerchief to his nose to disguise the smell. At the end of the corridor stood two policemen. His mind half registered the oddity – proceedings were complete and there was no reason for them to linger – before

---

[3] The Lord Chief Justice was one of the most senior judges in the country. The Lord Chief Justice in 1831 was actually Lord Tenterden, but (as far as I know) he was not the Grand Master of a villainous secret society.

dismissing it in favour of deep contemplation of a succulent piece of pork.

As he reached the policemen, one of them stood forward to block his path. Lord Walpole tutted beneath his breath in annoyance. Did they not know who he was?

"Excuse me, sir. Lord Chief Justice Walpole?"

"Well, evidently, that is me. Now would you kindly remove yourself from my path. I have important business to attend to."

"Lord Walpole, I have here a warrant for your arrest, in connection with the trafficking of human slaves. I fear your important business will have to wait for another day."

"But… but, this is preposterous! How dare you address me so. Do you think I am some common villain, to be subjected to the whims of a plodding policeman, such as yourself?"

"It's not for me to say whether you are either common or villainous, sir. That is for the courts to decide. My job is to arrest you and to place you safely into custody. So, if you would be so kind, to come with us, Lord – or should I say, Grand Master – Walpole?"

***

Kitty sat on the floor of the empty cobbler's shop, looking up as Mr Pounds toiled over the sole of a long leather boot. Jacob sat in the corner, silently observing them, while Charlie fidgeted nervously next to her.

"What about Polly? What about Flynn and the others?"

"I believe that Mr Pemberton invited them both to join you. However, they declined the offer. Apparently they felt they had more important things to attend to."

Mr Pounds continued.

"I am hoping, however, to prevail upon Polly, Flynn and their companions to attend lessons at my school. After all, who knows what such enterprising young people might achieve with the correct education. I even live in hope that I may prevail upon the two of you to join us. It has been some time since we saw you in classes."

Kitty looked down at her shoes and Charlie began to mumble.

"Sorry Mr Pounds."

When Kitty looked up again she realised his eyes were twinkling.

"I believe that you also may have had other, more important, matters to attend to. But thankfully, they are over, and you can now concentrate your inexhaustible energies on your learning. Mr Jacobs is proving to be an excellent teacher, and if I may say so, a great support to myself."

He smiled cheerfully.

"I'm sure that some of the children would rather attend his lessons than mine. Even over the last few days the school has become remarkably popular. As a matter of fact, Mr Dickens is talking about setting up a whole chain of 'ragged' schools across the country, for children such as yourselves. Imagine that! Education for everyone!"

His face gleamed with enthusiasm, and Kitty couldn't help feeling excited for him. Her face flushed red and she felt a sudden surge of emotion for this kindly man who had given so much of his time to help her. Mr Pounds dabbed briefly at his eyes with a yellowed handkerchief.

"Anyway, I forget myself. I am so sorry. I was carried away with the moment. So where were we?"

"You were telling us what would happen to the Scarlet Order."

"Ah, yes, well the Scarlet Order itself has been disbanded. Many of its former members have been arrested, and hopefully will stand trial."

"Hopefully? Surely they will all be locked away for a very long time?"

"One would hope so, one would hope so. But I fear, my dear Kitty, that it may not quite turn out that way. Some of these men are very powerful people, with great influence over the powers of justice. I fear they may yet escape judgement."

He glanced at Kitty and Charlie's downcast faces.

"Do not look so gloomy. Thanks to you, their involvement in the evil slave trade is over, and another blow has been struck for freedom and equality."

"And what of the slaves? Will they all be freed."

Jacob and Mr Pounds looked at each other, each seemingly unwilling to speak.

Eventually Jacob answered.

"No Kitty, I'm afraid it is not as simple as that. We have stopped the Scarlet Order, but they were only a small part of the picture. Still my people toil in captivity. British businessmen still ply their terrible trade in innocent people, and while those in power choose to turn a blind eye, they will continue to do so."

"So Philip was right. It was all for nothing!"

"No Kitty, it was not for nothing."

Mr Pounds' voice was quiet and soothing.
"We have fought for freedom and won a
battle. A small battle, maybe, but nonetheless
an important one. At this very moment,
slaves in the British colonies of the West
Indies are throwing off their chains and
seizing their freedom. Around the world
slavery extends its evil influence. It will stop.
It must stop. But we can only fight one battle
at a time."

Kitty looked at Jacob.

"When I left Jamaica, it was in chaos. We
had been promised our freedom for years, but
as season followed season it never came. The
law may have changed but wealth and power
had not. In the end, my countrymen took
matters into their own hands and rose up
against their masters. The fighting was brutal
and bloody as I left, and I was torn. While a
part of me yearned to join in the struggle, a
part of me was glad to escape. But I could
never escape the sense of betrayal. I felt that I
had let my countrymen down by not joining
their fight. So when Eliza offered me the
chance to do my part, I took it eagerly."

Jacob's face was hard to read. He held his
head proudly, but the eyes were mournful.
Kitty thought of what he had lost, what he had
suffered, and what he was suffering still. She

put out a hand and closed it softly over his, her fingers slipping gently into the folds in his roughened and blistered palms.

"What will you do?"

"I don't know yet. I have not seen my family in many years. I don't know even if they are alive. If my wife lives she may be remarried. If my children live they will be young men and women now, and their childhood will be lost to me. So I will try to find them, but I do not know where to start."

***

Jacob sat on the quayside, ignoring the cold that bit into his bones. He looked at the ships in the harbour, wondering which would be sailing to the warmer climes of his home. Not his home, he corrected himself. He had been pulled from his home as a young man, and now he was rootless, adrift in a world which still barely recognised his humanity. But still one of those ships might be journeying to where his wife lived - if she lived – and to where his children were now busy raising families of their own. Unbidden, the salt tears started to flow down the sides of his face, quickly washed away by the welcome rain.

He saw no future for himself here, but neither did he relish the return to Jamaica. He feared the voyage, and he feared what he would find when he got there. He had no wish to rejoin the flames and fighting. But England had brought him nothing but darkness, and of course the grey, miserable cold.

He thought of his former master, shamed and imprisoned. He felt no guilt, but a slight pang of pity. He had been well-treated, relative to some of his companions, but still he had no love for the pompous lords that had held him enslaved all those years.

Then he thought of Eliza Pemberton, and the anger ran coldly in his blood. He thought of her warmth in their few short conversations. He thought of her kindness and her concern for his safety. He thought of her lying, cold and stiff in the mud and felt the anger flood through him.

The anger gave him strength. It inflamed him but did not consume him. He felt suddenly certain, more so than ever he could remember, and he knew what he would do. He would return. He would find his family. He would find his peace.

***

Kitty hurried away from Mr Pounds' workshop. She was not sure where her feet would lead her, but she needed to think. With some surprise, she found herself back in Hampshire Terrace. As she neared the familiar frontage of number forty-three, her mind churned relentlessly, memories rising to the surface, before sinking once more into the mire. Something lay beneath that surface, hidden, elusive, but important. Could it be the key to the one remaining mystery, the thing that still bothered her, still niggled at the sides of her consciousness.

Who was Mr Peabody?

Nobody had seemed able to answer that question satisfactorily. Mr Pemberton had known him as a particularly unsavoury member of the Scarlet Order. But he knew nothing more about him, and that was where the trail seemed to end. Mr Dickens had tried to find out more but it appeared that he was utterly unknown to the authorities whose job it was to know such things. Jacob had shrugged his shoulders, indifferent to such details, as he came to terms with his new found freedom.

The winter sun glared off the white terraced walls, warming the chill air, despite the damp sea winds that whipped through the carefully spaced trees. Kitty was about to place her foot on the lower most step to the front door when a voice called out to her, bringing her up short.

"Kitty! Kitty! Over here."

It was Philip, walking on the grass on the other side of the road with his father. Kitty hurried over to them. Philip's eyes were bloodshot and reddened around the rims. Mr Pemberton's face was strained, as if in pain. As she approached, Philip shuffled his feet and would not quite meet Kitty's eye.

"Father and I, we were talking… we were talking about mother…"

His voice cracked and tailed off. Kitty put a hand on his shoulder. He placed his hand over hers and held tight for a moment. Then he forced a smile and cleared his throat noisily.

"How have you been Kitty?"

His voice was strained, and the question sounded unnecessarily formal. Kitty smiled sympathetically.

"I've been fine. Father and mother were at their wits' end with worry. When I got home I thought mother would never let go of me…"

Her voice trailed off as she realised what she had said, but somehow her words seemed to comfort Philip.

"It's ok Kitty. I'm glad your parents were so happy to have you back. They're lucky to have you."

He gave Kitty's hand an extra squeeze.

'And I'm lucky to have them.' Kitty's mind framed the unspoken words.

"We will be going back to London shortly Kitty. Father says he has much to attend to in the city. But we will stay in touch. And we will be back to Portsmouth soon. I promise you."

Kitty smiled weakly.

"I hope so. I really do. Please take care of yourself Philip. You too Mr Pemberton."

Mr Pemberton smiled down at her.

"Thank you Kitty. We will both take care of each other, I assure you of that. What of you though? You look troubled. What is worrying you?"

"Mr Peabody is worrying me. Who is he and where has he gone? How did he know Eliza?"

Mr Pemberton fell silent, pausing for a long moment. When he looked up his face was thoughtful.

"Samuel Peabody wormed his way into Eliza's confidence some years ago. Whether that was co-incidence, or all part of some intricate plan, I do not know. He passed himself off in society as an aristocratic gentleman adventurer. I think he appealed to the romantic in her. He filled her mind with tales of distant lands and battles for good against evil. She spoke of him to me, but I never met him. Of course I did not connect him with the dastardly Mr Chamberlain of the Scarlet Order. Why should I?

Who he actually is, we may never know. As Mr Chamberlain he was an industrialist and a member of the Scarlet Order. Who knows how many other characters and personas he may have? The more I have looked for him, the more any trace of him seems to vanish into thin air. But with the Scarlet Order finished I doubt he will return. What good would it do him? He will move on to more schemes and more villainous plans I imagine. Hopefully you will never hear from him again."

They were the words Kitty had been hoping to hear, but for some reason she experienced an unfathomable pang of disappointment. It was quickly dispelled as a familiar voice hailed them.

"Kitty! Philip! Mr Pemberton!"

She felt a welcome lurch in her stomach as Charlie's words filled her ears. She smiled as he ran over to them.

"Kitty, your Pa's asking for you."

He noticed the concern suddenly spread across her face.

"Nothing to worry about Kitty. He says he hasn't seen enough of you, and he wants us both to go back to yours for some food, to tell him all about our adventures."

Philip shifted awkwardly from foot to foot in the background.

"He said you could come too Philip. If you want to, that is."

Philip's beaming smile was answer enough. He looked up at his father, who nodded gravely. The three friends ran off towards Portsea, Kitty in the middle, flanked by the two boys. Mr Pemberton watched them go, until they had disappeared into the smog-blackened buildings beyond the fields. Momentarily the strained smile on his face gave way to the sadness and grief he could not show. Then he looked once more at the space where his boy had just been, running with his friends, for a short while forgetting his loss, and slowly, effortfully he turned away.

***

Joseph Chamberlain leaned back into the plush upholstery and smiled ruefully. He was not accustomed to being beaten. Particularly not by a couple of children. It had not been an entirely successful episode. Still, he had escaped with only the mildest of dents to his dignity and his fortune, which was more than he could say for the pompous gentlemen of the Scarlet Order.

He thought about Kitty Hawkins. She really was impressively resourceful, that girl. He sighed. He would have been better off if he had never involved her in the first place. How ironic that Samuelson and Bartholomew had found Eliza Pemberton before Kitty anyway. And yet, he could not be entirely sorry that he had met her. She had brought some interest and amusement into the whole affair. If nothing else he could salvage that.

He listened to the regular clicking of the carriage wheels on the cobbles. The journey would not be much longer. He would, of course, have to retire the identity of Joseph Chamberlain. It was a pity. It was an identity he had enjoyed. Bartholomew was dead. At least that loose end had been tidied up. Not as he had planned, but dealt with nonetheless. He was not overly worried about the capture of Mr Moseley. Mr Moseley knew well enough how to keep a secret. Besides, even Mr Moseley only knew him as Joseph Chamberlain.

He pulled from his pocket a silver pocket watch. Carefully inscribed on the lid were the words 'Christopher Richardson'. It was half past two. He would be arriving within the hour and would have much to do. He thought once more of Kitty. Somehow he had a feeling that their paths had not crossed for the last time.

The rhythm of the horses' hooves changed silently as the coach rounded a corner. He looked out at the familiar landscape, the rain-washed fields cloaked in the grey of morning mist. He pulled down the window and looked up at the coach driver.

"How are we doing, Bernard?"

"Nearly there Mr Richardson."

He smiled, and wiped away the last trace of Joseph Chamberlain.

THE END

And now for some history...

Kitty's Portsmouth

In 1831 Portsmouth was much smaller than the modern city. It mainly consisted of Portsea (the area around the dockyard), Spice Island (a notorious den of iniquity where sailors caroused in the many bars and pubs), and what is now known as 'Old Portsmouth' (the area around Penny Street, where Kitty and Charlie first encounter Samuelson and Bartholomew). As these areas became increasingly over-crowded the suburb of Croxton Town began to grow, initially with terraces of large houses, such as Hampshire Terrace and King's Terrace, where Kitty sold candles and investigated the identity of Joseph Chamberlain. Eventually, in the later nineteenth century, this suburb became known as Southsea.

Another new suburb, Landport, began to grow up to the north of the city and the fictional 'Flathouse Rookery' is placed, for this story, between the docks and Landport. This area was called 'Flathouses', although at the time it would have been barren land and fields between Landport and the Old Dock Mill.

The ruins of the Spur Redoubt, where Jacob was landed in captivity, still exist. It is thought that Admiral Nelson may have taken a boat from the Spur Redoubt to join his ship, HMS Victory, before the battle of Trafalgar. You can still explore the tunnel through which Kitty and Charlie followed Samuelson and Bartholomew that night.

Kitty's Portsmouth, though small, would have been busy and crowded. Sanitation was poor, which meant that the streets were dirty and smelly. Most of the population worked very hard for very little money, and disease was common.

Poorer children, like Kitty and Charlie, were expected to work for a living from a very young age. Most got little or no education, and Kitty and Charlie were lucky to get their free schooling from John Pounds.

Most of the locations in this story really existed, with the exception of the Flathouse Rookery, which is an artistic invention for the purpose of the story. Nonetheless, areas of Portsea were very crowded causing the population to spill over into Landport and other surrounding areas, including the Flathouses area near the docks. In 19th century England such areas of crowded deprivation were often referred to as 'rookeries'.

Lumps Fort

A key part of the action in this story takes place in Lumps Fort, which now forms the Model Village and Rose Gardens, near Canoe Lake in Southsea. This was originally built as a fortification to protect Portsmouth from attack from the sea. By the 1820s it had fallen out of use as a defensive fort, but continued to be used as a semaphore station until 1847. The fort stood near to the Great Morass, a large area of swamp to the south of what is now Albert Road, and covering the modern day 'Canoe Lake', through which Kitty and her companions pursue Mr Chamberlain at the end of the book.

The Slave Trade

Slavery underpinned large sectors of British business during the 18th and 19th centuries. Throughout this period millions of west Africans were enslaved and taken in British slave ships to America and the Caribbean, where they were sold, to labour in plantations. Their treatment was often brutal and barbaric and they were seen, not as people, but as possessions, to be used and abused by their 'owners'. Slaves lost their homes, their freedom, and even their names, which would often be changed by their 'owners' when they were bought.

In the late 18th and early 19th centuries there was growing opposition in Britain to the evils of slavery, from abolitionists such as William Wilberforce and Elizabeth Heyrick. Eventually, in 1807, Parliament passed a law to make it illegal for British people to be involved in the trading of enslaved Africans. Sadly this law was not well enforced and many British companies continued their involvement in the illegal but profitable slave trade. While the new law banned the trade in African slaves, it also did nothing to free those already enslaved.

The 1831 slaves' revolt in Jamaica, which features in this story, was instrumental in the eventual granting of freedom for Caribbean slaves. Led by Baptist preacher, Samuel Sharpe, it began with slaves refusing to work, in an attempt to force their owners to pay them to cut the valuable sugar cane harvest. It quickly escalated into violence. Slaves attacked plantations and seized land throughout Jamaica. Retribution was swift and British troops killed or captured hundreds of Africans, subjecting many survivors to vicious treatment. The violence and its aftermath shocked the British government into more actively pursuing an end to slavery. In 1833 the 'Emancipation Act' was passed by Parliament, providing for a gradual freeing of slaves in the West Indies, Cape Town, Mauritius and Canada, and in 1838 the remaining slaves in the West Indies were freed (ironically their 'owners' were compensated by the British government for the loss of their 'property'). Unfortunately, this new law did not ban slavery in other British colonies, and slavery in various forms continued in some areas of the British Empire until the early 20th century.

John Pounds

John Pounds was born in 1766 and trained as an apprentice shipwright in Portsmouth dockyard. After a fall into a dry dock, which left him with severe injuries, he became a cobbler, eventually setting up his own shop. He began teaching children in his workshop in St Mary's street, and gradually his classes grew in popularity, providing an education for many of the poorest children in the city. After his death in 1839 further free schools were set up in other parts of Portsmouth. John Pounds' work became an inspiration for the 'Ragged Schools' movement and for educational reformers who wanted to open up education to all children.

Charles Dickens and Portsmouth

Charles Dickens was born in Portsmouth in 1812 and his birthplace remains a museum to this day. Although he moved with his family to London in 1815, he remained attached to the city and made several visits in later life, as well as setting part of 'The Life and Adventures of Nicholas Nickleby' in Portsmouth. As far as I am aware there is no record of Dickens visiting Portsmouth in 1831, nor of him meeting John Pounds. However, Dickens, with his keen interest in education and his later involvement in the 'Ragged Schools' movement would have been aware of John Pounds and his work. In 1831, when this story is set, Dickens was a young reporter for the 'Mirror of Parliament'. He had not yet had any of his fictional work published and had achieved none of his later fame and fortune. Perhaps this adventure and his encounter with Kitty and Charlie inspired him to write some of his wonderful books…

Printed in Great Britain
by Amazon